FERAL
TEETH
PRESS

WEIRD TASTES FROM THE
El Cruz Seaside Diner

Feral Teeth Press
www.feralteethpress.com

ISBN: 9780692685099

First Printing

Cover & Interior Illustrations:
by Mat Fitzsimmons

WEIRD TASTES FROM THE
El Cruz Seaside Diner
BY MAT FITZSIMMONS

FOR BRANDI,
XOXO

El Cruz Seaside Diner

Specials*:

Appetizer
pg. 13

Breakfast Burrito
pg.23

Bloody Mary
pg.49

Mushroom Scramble
Pg.61

Hashbrown's Revenge
pg.75

Crispy Bacon
pg.95

Strong Coffee
pg.113

??? pg.169???

Eat It & Beat It

*Specials may cause nausea due to inappropriate preparation and/or unclean handling. Eat at own RISK!

!!! MENU ITEMS INTENDED FOR MATURE DINERS ONLY !!!
(selected items contain explicit ingredients)

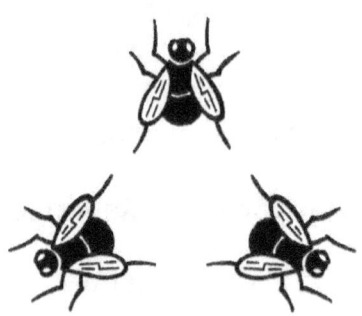

Appetizer

I'm going to try and explain how these stories came to fruition; fruiting bodies of work, like spores springing fourth from a tainted mind. I can't explain the titles, or where *that* idea came from; I'm not even going to try. I'll go in chronological order. It starts in one place, and sort of loops right back around; at least, in the funny sort of way that I look at things. And not, necessarily, funny as in, "ha-ha"; although, I hope you'll find a few of that variety in this collection, too...

So, where was I? Oh, yeah. During the summer of 1986, my then sleepy hometown of Santa Cruz, California, was transformed into a town called Santa Carla. This wasn't the first time that it had happened, either. A couple of years earlier, a guy named Dirty Harry had come to town!

Santa Cruz is a famous beach resort town known for its boardwalk. It's probably one of its most well-known attractions. Well, back in 1986 (pre- '89 Loma Prieta earthquake), downtown Santa Cruz was a *pretty* fuckin' bitchin' place. There used to be both a Rainbow Records, *and* a Double-Rainbow Ice Cream shop; Another place that *only* served baked potatoes, stuffed and piled high with your choice of fillings and toppings! I still almost get a tear in my eye, when I think about the Cooper House; I'm sure I'm not the only one. Then, way down in the seedy part of Pacific Avenue, there was the original Atlantis Fantasy World; Santa Cruz's first real comic book store. They've come a long way since that original location, although I think back on that old, blue wooden building, quite fondly. The smell, the squeak of the floors, the dim lighting...

I have a soft spot for gut-wrenching nostalgia.

So, back in that summer of 1986, I remember heading off to Atlantis Fantasy World to buy some Comics. Romita, jr.'s run on X-Men! When I pulled up to Atlantis, it looked as though some sort of gigantic (cyclopean!) construction project was in the works. There was a huge plywood wall, stretching up and down the entire length of the block. Upon closer inspection, it wasn't just a wall; it was more like a tunnel! Even though it looked closed, there was a sign that said, "comic book store open", or something along those lines. So, I locked up my Schwinn cruiser, and walked into the tunnel—

The inside of that tunnel had been built to give the appearance of being right there — amidst all the action — of the Santa Cruz Beach Boardwalk? There appeared to be all sorts of carnival-type game booths. Pop-a-Balloon. Circus-Punks... You get the idea. Santa Cruz Beach Boardwalk was almost a mile away as the crow flies! When I walked in to Atlantis, I'd asked the owner, Joe, what was going on. He'd told me they were filming a movie. The director wanted to give the appearance that Atlantis Fantasy World was actually a part of the hustle and bustle of the Santa Cruz Beach Boardwalk. If you look close, Joe is actually in the movie, sitting behind the counter. I remember thinking the whole thing was just too cool.

During that summer of '86, just before my 13th birthday, vampires roamed the streets of Santa Cruz! Well, not exactly Santa Cruz, but Santa Carla, the murder capital of the world!

It was even more thrilling still, when I saw those scenes projected upon the silver screen! I'd *been* there, in a place that didn't *really* exist; even if only for an hour or so...

As campy as it is, that movie is *still* one of my favorite horror movies of all time.

That movie is '*The Lost Boys*'.

Now, time-travel to 1993. One day, I was browsing a used book store, up the street from my parent's house. I've always loved to read, ever since I was a little boy, losing myself in the pages of stories. Mythology, fantasy, science-fiction and horror.

It took me a while, but eventually I *really* got into horror. Stephen King. I'm not fanatical, and I haven't read *everything* that Stephen King has written, but I've read a *lot* of it. The Stephen King stuff *and* Richard Bachman stuff. As it just so happens, one of my favorite stories of Mr. King's is a short story, '*The Mist*'. It turned out to be very relevant to the book I was holding in my hand, on that day back in 1993. I didn't know that at the time. Then again, I still had so much to learn...So on that day, back in 1993, when I'd picked up that book, the first thing I'd noticed was a blurb from Stephen King. He called the author the Master of Modern Horror; H.P. Lovecraft. Never heard of him—

I'd decided to buy the book.

Boy, oh boy...like most anyone that likes strange stuff who discovers the Cthulhu mythos, I ate that shit up! Outré settings; ancient forbidden books; strange rites, complete with alien incantations; weird old gods buried beneath earth & sea; things from outside space & time... It was like H.P. Lovecraft & crew were speaking directly to me. I was fascinated by the bizarre continuity of these tales—

There were, in actuality, a large community of writers contributing to the Cthulhu mythos. Along the way I discovered Robert Bloch, Clark Ashton Smith, Henry Kuttner, and Brian Lumley. I'd already been a fan of Robert E. Howard (One of my earliest cinematic memories is my mom and dad taking me to see *Conan the Barbarian* at the Skyview Drive-In. I was 9, bless their hearts) ... While there were many, many, other authors that have contributed to Lovecraft's great mythos, those were the authors that constantly seemed to thrill me the most with their bodies of work.

But, back to H.P. Lovecraft—One day my dad approached me, and asked what I was reading. I told him "This guy H.P. Lovecraft ". My dad's reaction was strange, sort of like he'd seen a ghost. He went on to tell me that H.P. Lovecraft had been one of *his* dad's favorite authors. At that point, I'd probably read at least two Lovecraft collections. It was like one of those *weird* familial twists from a Lovecraft story! I got chills down my spine. Although I was only eight or nine when my Grandpa Fitz passed away, over three decades ago, I vividly remember the stacks of pulp magazines next to his recliner. I didn't know, until later, that he'd been a sort of Lovecraft devotee. I was about 21 when I discovered Lovecraft, quite by accident, all on my own. When I read all those stories through my 20's and into my 30's, I felt as though I kind of got to know my grandpa, thumbing through those same stories he had read; maybe finding the same sense of mystery, dread and sheer excitement that he had. For this ability to feel like a kindred spirit to my late Grandpa Fitz, through *literature*, I will always have a soft spot for Lovecraft...In whichever strange and angled dimension he may dwell.

Somewhere along the way, I don't remember the year, but let's just say 2003 for storytelling's sake; one of my wife's co-workers turned us on to an author named

Christopher Moore. The book was called *Practical Demon Keeping*. It became a kind of lightning rod for my own work.

That book is Fucking Awesome!!! Here was a guy taking all of the same stuff I really dig about Lovecraft, and then blending it with an insane sense of humor. After reading more of his work, I found that Mr. Moore is capable of saying some very outrageous things. Anyone in doubt, need only read his wickedly hilarious vampire trilogy. I digress (though not terribly); back to *Practical Demon Keeping*….

One of the things that really struck me about that book, and stuck with me, was the setting. A small seaside town, somewhere south of Big Sur. The town in Christopher Moore's book is fictitious, but I could swear I'd been there before. I just know that I've visited *that* town; almost sure of it. A *few* times. I'm not going to name the town. It's fictitious, anyhow; although, I'm pretty sure something very close to it also exists in reality...Just like Santa Carla.

So I owe a special thank you to Stephen King, H.P. Lovecraft and Christopher Moore. Thank you!

This collection of short stories, Weird Tastes from the EL Cruz Seaside Diner, is my love letter to that forgotten Santa Cruz, or Santa Carla, of 1986 and other nonsense from my mischievous youth. If one were to believe in the multiverse, then El Cruz, Santa Carla & Santa Cruz are the same place existing in different dimensions. Enjoy!

Mat Fitzsimmons
2016

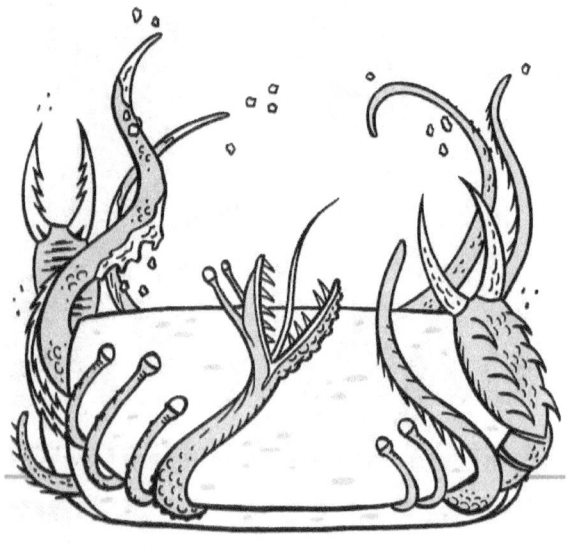

Breakfast Burrito

had quite a strange experience on the levy this morning. This is how things got *really* weird...

I'd worked the graveyard shift last night. As a stagehand you get used to working odd hours. We were breaking down gear for the dark wave band, "The Cadavers". Our crew really busted ass, wrapping it up early and calling it quits around 3 AM—

I recall waking up a bit groggy this morning, having only slept for about six hours. My stomach, grumbling, seemed to growl at me, "Hey Max. Wake your *ass up* and *feed* me! Now!!!"

Alright, Alright, I'm up already!

I'd sort of half strolled, half staggered down the hall, to the bathroom, to relieve Mr. Richard Johnson. My fantastic morning whiz commenced with two loud blasts of the butt trumpet; their reports echoing off the tile walls of the shower. Again, my gastrointestinal voice gurgled, saying, "I 've got some bad news, buddy, you'd better sit down for this one."

I took its advice...

Okey-dokey, then. With nature's business out of the way I'd quickly showered, brushed my teeth, and then finger-combed my hair. I'd returned to my bedroom, where I'd dressed in a flash, trying to ignore the one-way conversation my grumbling stomach was having with me.

As much as I'd tried ignoring my imaginary stomach-voice, it *eventually* opened up a line of communication with my subconscious.

"How 'bout a *breakfast burrito*?" My stomach asked my subconscious.

"*Yeah—and while we're at it, a big ol' cup of coffee!*" Subconscious enthusiastically responded.

Breakfast burrito and a cup of Joe. *Mmmmm-mmmmm.* Yeah, *now* I was in on the conversation! They were speaking my language...

I'd opened the drapes, peering outside, only to be greeted by muted light behind a dense gray marine layer; the ground wet from a thick drizzle. The past week had been unseasonably hot for October (*miserably hot, in fact*!), so, the mist was a welcome respite from the heat...Not to mention (although I guess I'm about to); I just happen to *love* foggy days in El Cruz. This particular fog looked thick and dreary; so it wasn't very likely that it would burn off soon, if at all. It was my favorite kind.

I've lived in El Cruz my entire life, and the place is one of the last bastions of cool. Separated by long stretches of abandoned coastline to the north and south; a mountain range to the east standing like an enormous fortress wall; and thousands of miles of

Pacific Ocean to the west, El Cruz and its neighboring towns are somewhat isolated on the northern-most part of California's central coast. El Cruz was founded in 1777 by Father Julio Serrano and houses one of California's Historic Missions. Although, now, it's known more for its beach boardwalk; radical surfing and skateboarding; loud underground rock bands; breakfast burritos, strong coffee and the All Mighty High-Grade Marijuana. But I digress, blah, blah, blah...

Any who, I'd grabbed a Mason jar, a quarter way full of the *OG Kush*, unscrewed the cap, and pulled out a nice knot of herb. I broke the sticky green nugget into three little pieces, appreciatively inhaling its skunky odor. After stuffing a piece into the bowl of my bong, I'd set flame to the small bud, inhaling its smoke to the gurgling-bubble sound of my water pipe. I packed up the next bowl, repeat; pack up the next one, repeat. That's what we called a *'Triple Expresso'*, around these parts, in the wake and bake community. I felt the herb's positive vibrations taking hold, right about the time I'd checked the clock. Quarter 'til ten!? It was time to *carpe diem*... You know, seize the day, and all that bullshit... *Time to get the fuck out of here*!

I'd grabbed my trusty Schwinn cruiser from the shed, rolling it through the backyard. In the driveway beneath the carport, I'd jumped on my bicycle, peddling off into the misty EL Cruz morning—

Geographically speaking, El Cruz has five parts of town. There's the Beach Flats, which is home to the infamous El Cruz Beach Boardwalk *(On a grizzly night in 1977, 13 people were savagely mauled in the boardwalk's Haunted Castle; several bodies mutilated beyond recognition. There were three survivors. The killer was never caught! This only heightened the seaside attraction's popularity with macabre thrill seekers.);* along with about 10 square blocks of low income housing. If El Cruz has a ghetto, it was definitely the Beach Flats. The main drag is the waterfront of a four block radius known as Squid Row.

From the irregular bowl shape of the Beach Flats, the elevation rises to about 30 feet from the shoreline and is divided by St. Lorenzo's River. This forms the east and west side of town.

The East Side is a warren of small beach cottages, one stacked on top of the next, creating a claustrophobic effect, with streets like labyrinths. It's local knowledge that many young tourist girls, and even a few local ones, were last seen entering those twisting alleyways of numbered avenues. Never to be heard from, nor seen, again.

The West Side is the older side of town with larger estate properties, many of which were crowned with weathered Victorian mansions, falling into several different categories of neglect. There are plenty of blue-collar type neighborhoods on the west side, too. With all the parks and open space, it's a desirable place for people to raise their families. But like every corner of El Cruz, the West Side wasn't without its dark secrets. Some of those old mansions, shuttered, boarded up, and long abandoned, were rumored to have been churches to strange and terrible things.

Pretty fucking cool, huh?!

Midtown is a small patch of neighborhoods that sits off the east bank of St. Lorenzo's River, including my own. Here, the flatlands begin to rise into the foothills of the El Cruz Mountains; the mountains themselves dense with age-old redwood forest. There are secret graveyards hidden in those mountains; burial sites of ancient tribes, and victims of meth-head biker gangs. More than one serial-killer has stalked those woods. Many, many more...

Downtown is three streets wide, running parallel with the river, and 10 blocks long. This is the place to: find neat trinkets, browse bookstores, catch a movie, drink cups of strong coffee, and/or grab a bite to eat. At night, it turns into a party atmosphere, with 10 different nightclubs that cater to as many different scenes: Goth Night at the Blue, metal at the Red Rum, punk bands at the Aquarium; Or, just the jukebox and cigarette-smoke-filled atmosphere of the seedier joints, like the Asti, or the Avenue. There was a G/L/B/T place called 'Koda.

At night, downtown El Cruz is lit by white twinkle lights. The lights are strung from the trees that line Oceana Avenue, illuminating a path for the swarming bar hoppers. Those same twinkle lights also lit that incident, 10 years ago, casting their magical, twinkling light, down upon *John Bishop; 52 years old, homeless, as he hacked off the head of Reggie Miller; 37 years old, homeless. With dozens of eyewitnesses, ranging from the slightly buzzed to the utterly shit faced, along with a small group of sober people coming out of a late-night movie, the police had no problem piecing together what had happened. Onlookers told officers how the two homeless men began arguing over religion, screaming back and forth for over three hours. This was confirmed by the late-night movie goers, who had seen the homeless men arguing on the way into the theater. As the argument became more heated, John Bishop was heard yelling at the top of his lungs, "XUSHATHULA WILL RISE AGAIN!!!"* Spectators said that he repeated this over and over, almost chant-like, before pulling a large machete from his backpack. Due to the eyewitness accounts, police estimate that it took somewhere between 5 and 9 strikes for Mr. Bishop to remove Mr. Miller's head! It had been a big story in town when I was young; like I said, *every corner of* El Cruz *has a dirty little secret.* Some weren't so secret, though...

Some were just dirty—

Alright. Enough about geography and macabre local history. Time for a big old cup of *coffee*! I hit the bike path that runs along the levy of the St. Lorenzo River, casually peddling my care-worn bicycle towards downtown El Cruz, aiming for Oceana Avenue.

I'm pretty opinionated about coffee (along with all kinds of other shit), favoring a strong flavorful cup. I drink dark roast, but not *French* roast. *Never French roast.* French roast leaves a bitter taste in my mouth. Nothing against the Frogs, I just don't drink their coffee! Hey, I know, opinions are like assholes. My asshole happened to smell like Pete's Coffee House, so that's where I was heading this drizzling October morning. All I could think about was a 24 oz. cup of their Zimbabwe blend. *Caffeineus Africanis*!

While cruising my trusty Schwinn along the levy path, I remember suddenly being struck with how absolutely quiet this particular morning was. I don't mean quiet in the sense of: No one out walking their dogs; No other cyclists commuting along this popular route; No young college girls out jogging, trying to combat that dreaded freshman 15 (lbs.). I don't mean quiet like that. It was like nature was holding its breath. Even on days when the sky is the color of dull lead, with raindrops falling as hard as stinging needles; the big black crows would be seen circling around overhead, cackling and cawing. The ever present seagulls should be screaming their high pitched calls. You couldn't go an hour without seeing a blue Jay or a gray squirrel. The same was said for stray cats, especially down by the levy, a natural feline fishing hole, full of fat rats... At that point, I was hoping to see a happy drunk wino...

There were none *of them*.

Further down the levy where the homeless encampments were located, I'd noticed an empty area just two days before that had looked like a thread-bare gypsy carnival. The cops *did* sweep the area a couple of times a year, although that seemed to always happen during summer time. Usually, El Cruz's homeless population would catch a tip, strike camp, and move it all a few miles up the river into the foothills. I'd guessed that was what had happened.

I'd been on the levy for about five minutes, and still hadn't seen any sign of life. After passing beneath the first bridge, I'd covered a quarter-mile of levy. Eventually, I came to the next spot where the path slopes downhill beneath the next bridge. The hill was fairly steep, as was the rise of the other side. I'd enjoyed the downhill glide, gaining momentum.

As I came to the flat space between hills, I'd cranked my Schwinn, picking up speed to aid in the uphill peddle. The morning was so quiet; I only heard the midrange hum of my bicycle's tires as I gained speed. Visibility, due to the thick marine-layer, was low. As I'd begun to pass beneath the bridge, I was hit with an overpowering stench. It was unlike anything I'd ever smelled in my life! It was like seven types of seafood; none of it fresh! The nauseating odor was tainted Oysters Rockefeller, served with toxic steamed clams; all caught on a red tide, then left to sit for a week! There was a wafting reek, that brought to mind, rancid cioppino... those smells, mixed with sushi that had gone off?! *Way off*! I also thought I caught a whiff of public wharf butcher-block, bait-bucket and tuna-fish sandwich that had been regurgitated... A word of friendly advice. If you encounter a seafood place that smells like this, you shouldn't even take a piss there.

That was when I'd gagged. I went into a full body shiver, dry heaving quickly; three times in a row. *Somehow,* I had managed to keep the trusty Schwinn upright. At least for a *few more* seconds, anyway. Those seconds seemed like hours, everything moving in slow motion.

O.K, this is where I think the story gets interesting—

After gaining control of my bicycle for all of three and a half seconds, I saw a dark shadow emerging in the fog up ahead... And I'm on a direct collision course with previously mentioned dark shadow! I stepped back hard on my Schwinn's coaster brakes, but, with my previous wobbliness, and both tires *and* path slick with the morning's drizzle. I went into a gnarly sideways slide. I slid for perhaps two seconds, every fraction of a second falling closer to the hard asphalt covered path. After what felt like a very long time, both body and bicycle slammed into the ground, sliding a few more feet to a painful stop. My trusty Schwinn lay atop my sprawled out figure. I'd quickly jumped to my feet, though, surveying the damage. Minor abrasions to my forearm and knuckles; a slightly larger one on the side of my knee; I'd live. But I didn't have to be happy about it. I was going to give this fuckin' troll a piece of my pre-coffee-mind! First, I had to shake off the pain, though.

As I was picking the Schwinn up off the path, the shadow-figure came into full view, emerging out of the mist. Suddenly, the thought of coffee and breakfast burritos were long gone; Along with any concern for my morning's caffeine fix.

Now, *El Cruz has a long, colorful list of some unsavory homeless characters,* but this dude had to take *the* fuckin' *cake!* Uhhm, alright, here we go:

The guy comes into view. I could just *tell* that the wretched smell was emanating from *him*. He's got to be, like, 75 years old, at the very least, but he's *ripped* like Iggy Pop. It's about 52° out, with the thickest drizzle you can imagine; and this *gnarly old geezer* is in a leather motorcycle vest, what could only be described as cut-off denim hot-pants, along with a pair of rattlesnake cowboy boots. He was also wearing a black cowboy hat, the sides turned up at extreme angles. Like a complete bad-ass. On his hatband (*also snakeskin*) was an ornament, wrought from green glass; glass that sort of looked like beach glass. It had been formed into the likeness of some ghastly sea serpent. His belt was black leather that appeared to have been wrought from the hide of a monstrous prehistoric fish, also studded with the strange looking sea glass. It was his belt buckle that made the most terrible impression upon me (*only speaking of his attire*), though. The thing depicted on that belt buckle was like a mollusk, but nothing like a mollusk; like an eel, but nothing like an eel. If I had to describe it, I would say that it was like a shark shaped man, wearing a spiked conch shell; with an octopoid head—although even that's not right—and as horrible as the creature was, the craftsmanship was amazing!

Its face had a dozen eyes, with a bat-shaped nose and lips like a fish; the things mouth was full of sharp barracuda's teeth. Its entire head was wreathed in gross *phallic* appendages! The creature seemed to be emerging from the protective shell; a shell that was somehow housing even *more* of that *hideous* monstrosity! Like his hat-ornament, the studs of his belt, a bracelet, along with a ring upon his finger, the dude's belt buckle was also intricately carved from the strange green glass. From a distance, this guy could have been the washed-up cadaver of some legendary heavy metal singer (*Lemmy Killmeister instantly came to mind*) ... Up close it was even worse—

Even though he stood with an extreme hunch, the dude was still well over 6 feet tall; rail thin, like a skeleton. Cords of grizzled muscle, along with strings of popping veins, stood out all over his leathery body! He reminded me of some great snake...

An albino python, maybe?

I'd dry heaved, two more times in succession, overwhelmed by his nauseating stench.

Gnarly old geezer, or Gog, as I've now began referring to him, wasn't what I'd call, like, a true albino; I don't know *what* was wrong with him. But it was definitely something. He was sort of a very, very, pale, *bluish* white. As a kid my dad would catch rock-cods that the Italian fishermen called Capazones. The bellies of these fish were a light turquoise blue, like a robin's egg. It was a beautiful color.

Gog was a *paler* shade of *that* color. Not so pretty on a man. I think there's a good chance Gog had been a sideshow freak at some point in his lifetime.

His *whole body* seemed to be tattooed in fish scales, a slightly darker color than his own skin; aquamarine whirls and spirals covering his upper chest, arms and legs. Running along the sides of his arms, legs, and then like a collar around his neck; strange symbols of bright fluorescent orange that seemed to *glow* in the dreary morning light. It's funny, but full body and face tattoos just aren't *quite* as shocking as they *used* to be. *Especially* not in a place like El Cruz. On the other hand,

Gog's ink was *extremely* well done, lending the owner the aspect of some fierce creature from a grim old fairytale. Besides the horrendous smell and weird appearance, there was something just very off putting about this gnarly old geezer...

I know it's taken me a while to describe Gog up to this point. At the time, I'd made all these observations in about 10 seconds. Then I'd taken a good look at his face! *Holy Fucking Shit*!!! Gog's face was drawn and haggard, covered in wrinkles, and scale-tattoos. His nose was close to his face, the nostrils gaping wide. Around his mouth there were four long, translucent skin tags that made me think of a catfish... *And that mouth*?

Gog's lips were extremely thin, his mouth extraordinarily wide. The mouth of an amphibian! Or a geek, maybe. His lower jaw was jutting-out in a slight under-bite, exposing teeth that looked like they'd been filed to savage points! I'd looked into Gog's eyes and my heart skipped a beat—I mean really skipped a fuckin' beat—because at that moment, I realized something was terribly wrong with Iggy Creep *(another nickname I've since come up with)*. His eyes were spaced a bit too far apart, and were much too large for his face. They bulged outwards, and I remember comparing them to Ping-Pong balls. *Gleaming white Ping-Pong balls*, popping from Iggy's eye-sockets. No iris; no pupil. He blinked, transparent membranes closing and then retracting, where eyelids would've been—should've been—on a human face! I caught him looking me up and down, as he smiled. When I'd first seen Gog's bulging milky eyes, I'd been sure that he was blind. *But those terrible eyes saw me! His* smile *told me that...*

And his smile? It made that hideous face even more so, exposing upper teeth, as sharp as his lower ones. Now, an entirely different thought entered my mind; Gog had gone from *hideous* to *dangerous*. In nature, teeth like that were only found on predators. Gog was like no other creature I've ever seen. He definitely didn't seem like anything from the natural world! Not with those chompers...

As scary as his shit-eating grin and sharp jagged cannibal's teeth were, I somehow kept focusing back on his eyes. Almost, like, I don't know how to describe it, other than against my will.

Another foul wave of his putrid smell washed over me, snapping me out of the momentary daze! Had he been *trying to hypnotize* me? How long had I been *standing* there *gawking* like a fuckin' *idiot*? I think he was, in a weird way, *hypnotizing* me!

I'd broken direct eye contact and focused on his forehead (*thankfully his least offensive feature*). I wasn't sure how long it took me to make these observations; it was as though the world stood frozen in time. Then Gog broke the absolute silence.

"What are you looking at, *punk*?" Gog croaked. It literally croaked, the Thing's voice sounding like a cross between a gigantic bullfrog and my gurgling bong.

After hearing Gog's voice, I began thinking of Iggy Creep as a "*Thing*", and an "*It*", instead of a man.

Gog was definitely monstrous. Up until then, I only knew the half of it.

What in the Fucking Hell!? The smell was like something from the pits of the Netherworld!

"Well, uh, I...um...er. Nothing. Sir?" I'd barely managed to stutter out, somehow turning my answer into a question. Yeah. I was really letting Iggy have it...

"Well, uh, I...um..." The Thing's croaking voice, mocking me, before barking into a coughing fit. A wretched wind from the bowels of Gog had blown upon my face... I could almost fucking taste it...

Gog's breath *pummeled* me! Bait squid, anchovies, dead seal and decomposing kelp; all of it rotten. All of it vile. If I'd had anything in my stomach, I would've vomited then and there. As it was, I'd dry heaved three more times, each time more violent than the last. On the final retch, I had a full body spasm, dropping my trusty Schwinn. I'd scrambled to pick my bicycle up, everything seeming to take much longer than it should have. Gog spoke again:

"You're *lucky* I already ate *my fill* this morning, *worm*!" The Thing stood up to It's full height, bones and cartilage making audible popping noises. Iggy *Pop* indeed! Fully erect (*no, not like that! Get your mind out of the gutter*), Gog was like, 6'10"!

"*Sir*?" It croaked again. Mocking. "*More like* Sire..." Gog's voice managed to hiss and boom at the same time, bouncing off the enclosed concrete walls.

I'd begun walking backwards. "Look man! I'm just trying to get some coffee and some breakfast... I'm not lookin' for trouble."

I had continued to back up, hoping to put another 10 feet between us, before turning to make a mad dash. In the next instant Gog took one large loping step forward, closing the gap between us. Its face wrinkled and contorted in anger. Then the Thing raised Its hoary voice. I could feel the bass of Gog's words, vibrating deep inside my chest. At this point, I'd like to say that I'd only had butterflies in my stomach, but that would be putting it lightly; making me even seem almost macho. I'd harnessed every bit of nerve I had just to keep from shitting my pants!

"I didn't dismiss you, worm!! Do you find me so offensive? For one not looking for trouble, trouble certainly seems to have found you! I am Zerathrux; a favored Herald of Kr'lyrus—third born daughter of *Xushathula*!" Its voice rumbled, "*Xushathula,* who has for all of humankind's history and so much longer, dwelled in the watery depths!" It made a series of strange hand gestures that seemed to indicate some sort of ritual or something, pointing out towards the direction of the Pacific Ocean. Like, Tai Kwon Weird!

Whoa!!! Wait a minute! This creep just mentioned *Xushathula*— that was a name I recognized, and the last time some homeless fucker started bellowing about this *Xushathula*, things ended in more than a verbal tongue lashing... *It was time to bail this scene, and quick*!

"On your knees and grovel, worm!!" The Thing bellowed.

I didn't think I could out run Gog. I had slowly been backing up the entire time. I'd managed to put about 25 feet of space between us. I was beginning to have a hard time walking backwards *and* pulling my bike... because, I'd realized, I had walked almost halfway up the incline of the hill that I'd originally descended.

"Oh, *I'm going to make you* pay! You *insolent little* punk!!!" The Thing spat out. It was smiling a deadly smile. Gog pointed Its finger at me. That's when I'd really noticed It's hands. Its fingers were long and slender; there was a thin membrane of flesh connecting them up to the last knuckle! And Its *fingernails—* the Thing's fingernails *—were like the talons of a Komodo* Fucking *Dragon!*

I might not be able to out run Gog, but I was pretty sure I could out-fuckin'-ride the Thing. My trusty Schwinn was on the right-hand side of my body. Good. I had dared a quick glance down at the sprocket of my bicycle, paying particular attention to the position of the pedals. Perfect.

My attention snapped back to Iggy Creep, as I'd heard another series of weird noises:

There was another crackling sound of bone grinding against cartilage, accompanied by a low rumbling growl that was building up in Gog's chest. The Thing underwent *a hideous* transformation!!! Gog was now easily over 7 feet tall; the only parts of Iggy Creep's body that had grown where It's *terribly* elongated neck, and puffed up *blow-fish* chest! I'd clearly been able to spot what could only have been Gog's gills. Three per side, each one pulsating, open and shut, in time with the rise and fall of the Thing's chest... The growl was rapidly rising to a roar!

I'd secretly wished that Scooby and the gang would pull up in the Mystery Machine...

Momentarily frozen in terror, I couldn't help but notice Gog's face, which had also changed. The Thing's bulging milk-white eyes shifted further to the sides of It's now pushed forward face. The bridge of Gog's nose had almost disappeared completely into It's weird face, leaving only huge gaping nostrils. Gog threw Its head skyward and roared, exposing a maw of daggers. Gog no longer reminded me of a *snake*... *No, It was something entirely* different *now*... It was like *an eel*!

A Wolf-Eel!!!

The roar snapped me out of my daze—O.K., fuck this noise—time to roll! I'd stepped down hard on the left pedal, throwing my right leg over the frame of my Schwinn. At that moment, I was like a cowboy mounting his horse in an old western movie. I'd tucked in low to the wide handlebars of my cruiser, peddling like a bat out of hell, aiming right at the gnarly old fucking Thing! "Get the fuck out of my way Fish-Face!" I'd screamed at the monstrosity as I barreled down upon It, gaining momentum and speed. We were locked in a game of chicken (*Chicken of the Sea, motherfucker!*). If I swerved, I was going down. And I had no doubt Iggy Creep would be on me; On me, like a fly on shit. With It's *horrible* teeth. *Teeth like razor-sharp little* knives!

I'd shuddered...

If Gog jumped out of the way, I'd have a clear shot up the hill on the other side of the bridge. I would still have to pump my bike uphill about two thirds of the way, but I was pretty sure Gog wouldn't catch up to me by then. There was *no way* I was swerving. *If I was going down, I was taking this hellish creature with me*!

The determination must've shown on my face, because about two seconds before impact, Gog slithered aside. As I wheeled past the Thing, It turned in a wide arc towards me, Gog's eel-like neck, and then It's head striking out at me! Now, Iggy Creep's mouth was that of a shark, the Thing's jaws extending out and away from Gog's head; *row upon row of* terrible teeth!! As the horrible creature barely missed, I'd screamed, "Jesus Christ!"

Gog chuckled, if such a Thing can truly chuckle, and said, *"Oh, that one has nothing to do with this—* Nothing *what so ever—"*

I'd felt a slight scratching across my shoulder blade. The Thing had just raked those *velociraptor claws across my fucking* back! The stench of 100,000 dead anchovies rotting in the sun, washed over me. And then, in an instant, I had passed the wretched Thing!!!

My momentum took me almost half way up the other side of the hill. Twelve frantic rotations of the sprocket finished the job. As I reached the top, I'd heard Gog's voice echoing out from below the bridge. It croaked, taunting:

"And haven't you heard? Jesus has been dead for over 2000 years. My mistress, the goddess I worship, *Kr'lyrus*, was born over *1 million years ago*! And perhaps one day, if you're lucky, if you kneel and grovel, you too may worship before the *thousand tentacles of Kr'lyrus*..."

From the echo of It's voice beneath the bridge, I could tell that the Thing wasn't pursuing me. I'd cranked the sprocket 20 more times (*or so*) up to a bend in the levy path, where I'd applied my coaster brakes, tires skidding to a halt. From this vantage point, I could see Gog's silhouette against the gray sky. Once more, Gog had assumed the shape of a man.

"And *Xushathula*? She is one of The Seven Queens of the Rim of Fire! Asleep in her prison of H'fuu'Aru, She was born over *five million years ago*. It has been written, in forbidden books, that the Seven Queens shall one day rise from the depths of the sea and earth to *enslave* mankind. Making way for their gods! The *Lords of Outer Darkness*." Its voice reverberated, "In those millions of years, the Queens have been lying in wait, cursed with minds that know of all that has been *and all that will be*. They remember *everything* about all of humanity's man-gods. Things your people will *never*, ever *relearn*. Yessss," Gog's voice hissed again, all the more monstrous coming from something that walked in the guise of a man. "Even Jesus!"

The Thing scaled over a retaining wall, scrambling down a section of river bank that no human being could have climbed, all with the ease of a salamander. At a small ledge, that could only be accessed by the creature's maniacal downward climb,

Gog quickly removed It's clothing, stripping off It's hat, vest, belt, boots and short-shorts (*thank God I witnessed this at a distance, mercifully saving me from an eyeful of mutated Trouser Trout*); then stuffed It's clothing into a crevice. Iggy Creep looked in my direction, although now I was about a hundred yards away. "*See you* soon... *punk*," the Thing crooned in a sandpapery sing-song voice, before plunging headfirst from the ledge into the river, some 10 feet below. Once in St. Lorenzo's River, the strange man-creature began swimming in my direction. I'd gasped at how smooth — how fluid— and how fast, Gog's body knifed through the water. In an instant, It was at the bend in the path where I sat astride my Schwinn, looking up at me with those horribly blank, Ping-Pong-ball-like eyes. I'd felt myself being drawn into those disgusting milky orbs; once again, it was like I was being hypnotized, Gog looking deeper and deeper into my soul. Then:

"See you soon," It mouthed. If Gog had spoken (*or croaked, growled, even hissed*), it didn't seem that I'd heard actual words. More like a voice swimming in my head. I peeled my eyes away from those terrible Ping-Pong ball eyes.

The Thing swelled up It's massive chest with a mighty inhalation of breath, submerging into the brackish river-water, to begin Its nightmarish submarine voyage towards the sea.

"Not if I can help it," I'd exhaled out loud.

From my vantage point, not only could I see the bridge and ledge from which Gog had jumped; in the other direction, I could see down to the river's mouth, where it met the Pacific Ocean about a mile and a half away. I also had a view of the looming silhouettes of El Cruz Beach Boardwalk's amusement rides; standing like giant alien invaders towering in the coastal fog, silently waiting to take the little tourist town by storm.

The river was slow-moving and as smooth as a sheet of glass. I'd sat there on my trusty Schwinn for another 3 to 5 minutes or so. In that time, not once, was there a ripple upon the water. Nothing disturbed it. Nothing broke the surface... It was just still and gray, reflecting the leaden sky. And all that time, Gog *never* resurfaced for air. *Not even once*...

The shrill cry of a seagull brought me out of my stupor. I'd watched as the gull flew down beneath the bridge, landing atop the retaining wall on the other side of the St. Lorenzo River. Within a few moments, it was as if the world had come alive...

A cyclopean Volvo station wagon (*one headlight was burned out*) drove over the bridge, heading towards Downtown. It came to a screeching halt on the wet pavement, stopping at a red light. The dilapidated station wagon was pulsating, rattling to the bass of some dance-hall reggae. Inside, a young white kid with natty dreadlocks puffed on a joint the size of my finger. Three big crows cawed at me as they came flapping up to the bridge, perching themselves on the handrail. It was almost as if they were saying, "BEAT IT DUDE, this is *our spot*!"

The traffic light turned green. The Volvo, buzzing with blaring reggae music, quickly disappeared into the morning mist. And then, as if to add insult to injury; the seagull from the other side of the levy flew overhead, a large chunk of what could only have been the "roach" end of a breakfast burrito, clamped firmly in its beak.

'At least the scurvy sky-rat didn't feel the need to shit on me,' I'd thought.

I'd been wrong. The fucking filthy-dirty, scurvy-fuckin' sky-rat *had* felt the need to shit on me. I wish I'd had an Alka-Seltzer to feed him...

Severely shaken, I'd begun peddling the trusty Schwinn back home. My world had *drastically* changed this morning. I'd seen something mortal man is not supposed to see. I had stared into the abyss, and the abyss had stared back.

I could always brew a strong cup of coffee at home, I guess. And my *appetite*?

Oh, *I'd lost my appetite*

So much for a breakfast burrito...

Bloody Mary

L ots of towns seem to have a White Lady. Not in the sense of a Caucasian woman; a White Lady in the sense of a spirit. A ghost. A phantom.

El Cruz was no different. White Ladies more often than not are young woman, barely out of girlhood, struck down in the spring-time of their lives. They are all waiting for the distant return of some far off lover. The White Lady is almost always a widow. El Cruz's White Lady was no different. Her parents named her Mary Elizabeth Waite. She grew up a happy girl during her childhood, for the most part.

The Waite family was an honest, hard-working family. Mary's father was a fisherman. Mister Waite *just* managed a comfortable life for his brood, but barely. This was no small feat in El Cruz County during the early 1930's.

In May of 1939, Mary Waite turned 15; which was courting age. As it turned out, Mary had caught the eye of Percival Montgomery, the Third; oldest son of one of El Cruz County's wealthiest families during that era. It certainly didn't hurt that Percy, as Mary would come to call him, was filthy rich; but he was also very handsome. Percy was quite a dashing fellow. During that era, Percival would've been what they called a 'catch'. On top of that, Percy was kind, charitable, and philanthropic. It was no wonder that Mary Elizabeth Waite, who'd grown up her entire life in the Beach Flats of El Cruz (far rougher in the 30's & 40's than now), had fallen, head-over-heels in love, with the wonderful Percival Montgomery, the Third. And he in turn, had equally fallen for her, despite her lower station in life. They had been courting for 2 years, when on the night of their anniversary, Mary gave Percy her flower. She was 17 years old. The night was December 6th, 1941. The following day, the Japanese bombed Pearl Harbor. Percival Montgomery, the Third, being above all a patriot—he was nothing if not a patriot—marched down to the nearest recruiting station and joined the Navy.

Within a year, Percival was flying a bomber, a handful of successful sorties under his belt. Percy was well on his way to becoming a war hero...A year after that, Captain Percival Montgomery, the Third, was shot down over the Pacific Ocean. No wreckage was ever recovered; Percival's body was never found—

Knowing of Percival's deep love for Mary, and realizing his son's intentions, should he have returned from the war, Percival's father gave Mary Elizabeth Waite a house by the sea. To this day, it's the *only* house on the ocean-side of El Cruz's rugged Westside coast. It was in this house; overlooking the vast Pacific

Ocean, that Mary Waite began her vigil; her *madness*; her remaining days...

***

As became her ritual, Mary would sit and look out the great bay windows over the mighty Pacific, watching the stars twinkle to life overhead. There was something strange about those windows, though. Upon the first star of evening, every evening for 365 straight nights; Mary wished upon that star.

And so it was for another 365 nights. Except on this year, Mary had stumbled upon some strange books bundled together in clusters, up in the attic. Why she'd gone up there, she couldn't remember. It's not like they were blasphemous manuscripts or forbidden tomes...in fact they weren't even *books* at all. They were magazines, really. Pulp magazines; most bearing the same title; Weird Tales, though there were others, too. Mary began to read about undersea creatures, great and small, in the pages of these stories. She read of Gods; sleeping under the ocean, waiting to rise. These authors were writing about the stars, too; how things, even people, could come back into being, cheating death, when those stars were right. "That is not dead which eternal lies, with stranger aeons even death may die..." became Mary's mantra that year. The year was 1945.

Mary sat by those gigantic windows, those strange portals, watching magnificent sunset after magnificent sunset. She never saw the beautiful, ever-shifting spectrum of yellow, orange, pink and red. Mary Waite only saw shades of purple, when that first star would flash into being.

Waiting to make her wish; the one constant yearning wish. 'Oh, Percival,' Mary thought. The great bay windows magnifying her aching energy...

This went on for seven years, from first wish to last. And on that last night?

A 26-year-old Mary Waite, malnourished and wasted to near nothingness, sat looking out to sea; she was completely blind to the swirling colors of the fiery sky, as day so surely surrendered to night. She was like an Old Maid, having never known the touch of another man. Only Percy's gentle embrace; those tender kisses, the eventual penetration, on that distant night of December 6th, 1941. Mary saw the sky go from a velvety violet, to a majestic purple. Her heart fluttered in her frail chest. Mary groaned, the sound husky in her throat. She saw the first star ignite in the heavens. Mary Elizabeth Waite made her wish. The strange windows amplified the widow's emotions, sending them out into the night, and beneath the surface of the jade green sea. The sky turned from eggplant to indigo, stars scattered across the night. Mary didn't see those stars, though; those stars didn't count when it came to making wishes...

So on *that* night, Mary fell asleep while reading a shudder pulp; one she'd picked out from the huge stacks of magazines she'd found in the attic. She had become an avid reader of these found pulp fictions.

Especially the weird stuff. She liked a little bit of spooky romance stuff, too; *Spicy Mystery*, when she was feeling lonely. And there was no shortage of the things. Mary had found over 500 pulps, all sorts of lurid titles, up there. Tonight she was reading *Weird Tales*. It was a spooky story by the author Henry Kuttner. He'd become one of her favorite mythos authors, when she would come across his work; along with Clark Ashton Smith, Robert E. Howard, and of course, H.P Lovecraft.

That night, Mary dreams of a cyclopean city, beneath fathoms of black water. Eventually she comes to a place lit in the phosphorescent light of the deepest sea. She is naked. She can feel the pressure crushing her chest, popping her eardrums, forcing her eyeballs from her skull. Despite the incredible pain, Mary can still see. The only sound is the sound of the abyss. A strange, nearly-silent sound... but still a sound none the less.

This place she has come to was built from bizarre angles, and unsettling geometry. Mary finds herself floating before an enormous bas-relief wall depicting some horrible entity. From a tiny fish-scale of that terrible entity, illuminated from within, a figure emerges; the man shaped (Percival?) silhouette, swimming up and up; staying close to the monstrosity of the monument, a mere speck upon the gargantuan wall. Mary follows the swimmer, her eyes now adjusted to the inky darkness. They swim up and up; for how long she can't tell. It's a long, long time... and while the pain is still there, Mary is oblivious to it. She's too terrified by the face of the beast on the bas-relief, as they swim up and away from the thing. Only hints of the creature are visible in the undulating underwater light. She hears and *feels* a name; A pressure in her body. In her head...Zushakon! Thank God she can only catch quick glimpses. As horrible as the monument is, it's merely a depiction, and not the actual deity. Mary follows the solitary swimmer on his upward swim; following his phosphorescent glow. They break the surface, swimming to the sandy cove below Mary's house. In the light of a golden full moon, Mary can tell the creature is some ichthyic thing. Some man-fish hybrid; but a thing with Percy's eyes! Mary thinks he's magnificent; an angel from the deep, his grey flesh shimmering like a Fire opal. Mary dreams that the creature's huge flaccid penis, hanging between his legs and swinging like a pendulum, suddenly grows hard! It takes her breath away...

She dreams that the Percy-thing mounts her, thrusting his now frightening, erect manhood in and out of her swollen entrance. The fish-man unlocks unknown doors of passion; Percival Montgomery, the Third's, eyes staring out from the body of Oannes; of Neptune; of Dagon! The Percy-fish-man-thing rises just before dawn, leaving Mary exhausted.

Mary awoke late the next morning. She was naked. She felt damp, as did her bed. Mary Waite's fingers were thrust deep up inside her aching crotch... All of it a dream. Or was it?

***

3 months later, Mary Waite was as ripe with child as any woman in her 9th month of pregnancy. And it's that pregnancy which turned Mary Elizabeth Waite, El Cruz's White Lady, into *our* version of Bloody Mary. I know other places are famous for their Bloody Mary's. This just happens to be *our* town's version. And she *is* a spicy one...

***

At home, while watching the heaving sea, Mary Waite went into labor. An unnatural labor; giving way to a horrific birth! Mary pushed and pushed, the legs of some giant, pre-historic frog-thing, kicking; came tearing out from her opening. The Percival-fish-man's son, insisted upon a C-section, using a razor sharp claw to slice through its mother's belly. The baby finally wiggled itself out of Mary's torso; her screams drowning out the sound of bones breaking, as her fish-baby forced itself completely out of her. Mary was still conscious as her love-child took its very first bites. The baby nourished itself on his mother's corpse, stripping flesh from bone; a piranha child. When it had eaten its fill, leaving tattered strands of skin and cloth, the fish-baby returned to the safety of the mighty Pacific Ocean. If it stuck to the shallows for a few decades, it might grow up to be a majestic thing, indeed!

Of course Mary Elizabeth Waite, her corpse a bloody, ravaged cadaver, had been wearing white.

They're always wearing white...

***

No one has stayed all that long in the house on the cliffs, overlooking the sea. People who have rented it as a vacation house from time to time report having the fright of a lifetime. Sometimes, just after the sun sets, on nights when the constellations are arranged just so, visitors to the Mary Waite house will see her reflection in those strange gigantic windows. She's nearly cracked in two from side to side, her ribs jagged, broken from the inside out. The little bit of flesh left on her body's bones hung like bloody, tattered, rags, along with the shredded cloth of her dress. But her face, head, and hair, were all left untouched.

Beautiful. Immaculate.

She would always cry for both Percival and Alexander, before evaporating into green witch-fire. And every seven years, an occupant staying at the Mary Waite house would seem to go missing. Permanently. People around these parts, the El Cruz locals, speculate on those disappearances. Most figure those that went missing received a visit from Percival, the-fish-man-thing. And—they always quickly add—if it isn't Percival, then it's most certainly Mary's son; Alexander...

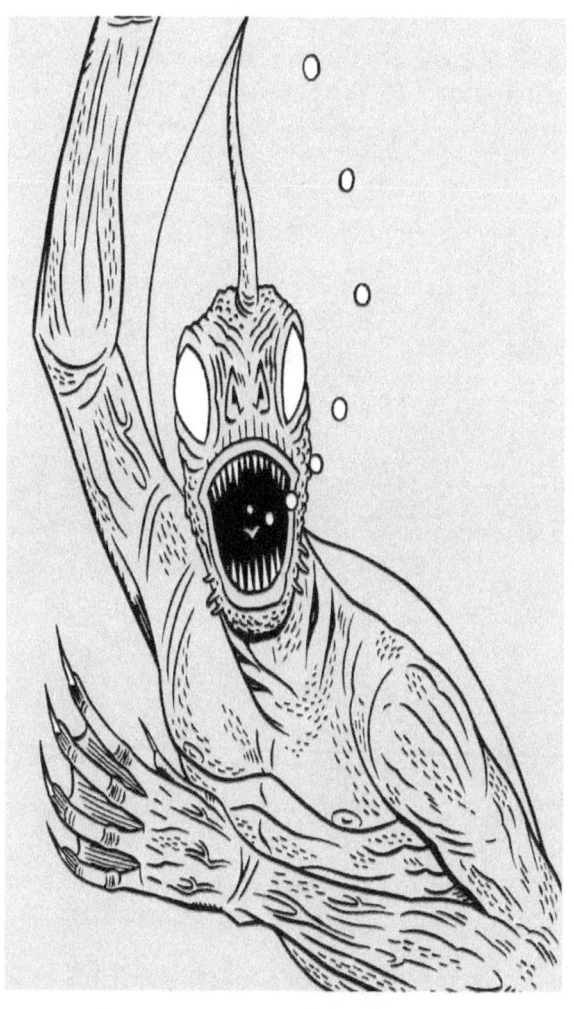

Mushroom Scramble

C harlie loved mushrooms. It's not like you're thinking, though. Sure, he'd gone through his hallucinogenic phase during culinary school. That was over a decade ago; twelve years, if we're keeping track of time. Now, Charlie was pretty much grown up. He was a full-blown adult.

Besides being an adult, Charlie Meyers happened to be the owner/chef of the hottest breakfast joint in El Cruz, California. Voted 'Best Breakfast Restaurant' 8 years in a row. From one wall of windows, 3 lucky tables of 2 caught a glimpse of the Pacific Ocean. He'd named the place Occult Omelet, after his signature dish, and, his love of the supernatural. Charlie's restaurant only sat 16 people; the interior decorated like a gypsy fortune-tellers lair. The food was excellent, and the coffee strong; Occult Omelet served nearly a hundred meals a day, 6 days a week (closed Mondays in observance of The Order of Xushathula). With the exceptions of Walpurgis Night, All-Hallows Eve, along with the summer and winter solstices, Occult Omelet served breakfast from, "7 AM 'til 12 noon every day of the year", as the sign in the front window declared.

Charlie had a strong work ethic. He was also insistent upon using only fresh, local ingredients. It was the mushroom-potato-bacon hash, that kept Charlie's costumers coming back morning after morning for more. Every day after work, Charlie would take a hike in a grove of nearby coastal redwoods, picking wild mushrooms. He'd recently published a book. It had made it onto the New York Times Bestsellers list, making Charlie Meyers El Cruz's premiere celeb-u-chef. His menu was deceivingly simple, as follows:

Occult Omelet

All breakfasts served with mushroom-potato-bacon hash; two slices (4 pieces) home-made toast; choice of coffee or tea. No substitutions, please.

Occult Omelet
(Some things in life are secret. Enjoy!)
$15

Bizarre Benedict
Two eggs (poached), seared ahi, lobster hollandaise on a sourdough English muffin. Fresh tomato slices in place of toast.
$13

Strange Scramble
Two eggs (scrambled), extra-sharp Cheddar cheese, seasonal grilled mushrooms, avocado, sausage patty crumbles, and green onions.
$13

Fearsome French Toast
Homemade, thick-cut raisin bread; soaked in rum and egg-nog. Served with powdered sugar, butter, bananas, macadamia nuts and real maple syrup. Bacon or sausage patty in place of toast.
$13

Create Your Own Monster (Scramble or Omelet)
3 eggs; choice of 4 veg, 1 meat and choice of cheese:
$15

Veg: Seasonal mushrooms, white onion, green onion, bell pepper, jalapeno, olives, tomato and avocado

Meat: Bacon, sausage patty, ham.

Cheese: Extra-sharp Cheddar, Monterey Jack, Monterey Pepper-Jack, Swiss, white American or Feta.

Charlie took pride in the fact that he served big, hearty, and above all, delicious meals to the good people of El Cruz. In return, the community had given him a thriving business, a house he called his very own, and most important; a sense of community. El Cruz was the place that Charlie Meyers was going to plant his roots; a place he could really keep growing. El Cruz had provided Charlie with a comfortable existence, down by the sacred sea.

Today happened to be a rare Friday off, being All-Hallows Eve. Charlie always observed the days when the veil was thin; when the old gods could, and would, hear the devotions of mankind (no slight on womankind; females are much more sensitive than males. In covens, they have up to 24 opportunities a year to convene with the old gods). Charlie prayed to Xushathula, one of the Seven Queens of the Rim of Fire. She sleeps imprisoned in a great vault, in one of the deepest places in the Pacific Ocean. She dreams; sealed behind a gigantic portal inscribed in protective charms that glow with orange fire.

Charlie was taking the morning off, 'Praise Xushathula!', and cooking *himself* breakfast for a change. On his hike, yesterday afternoon, he'd come upon some *really* exotic mushrooms. Even though he'd seen mushrooms like this, he'd never really seen ones *quite* like this. They were semi-transparent, resembling milky blue glass when held to the light. Purple veins climbed the stalks, spreading out over the mushrooms caps. The caps were decorated with a psychedelic dot pattern, of marigold, and bright electric blue. When Charlie had picked the mushrooms, the mottled light of the forest had played tricks on his eyes. The psychedelic dot patterns seemed to be pulsating with an inner light; until Charlie would pick them. Then the glow would die out. Another peculiarity Charlie noticed was that as soon as he'd picked them, the mushrooms turned semi-opaque; a creamy blue-yellow color. Not *quite* the color, of almost every edible mushroom he'd ever seen, or eaten. Charlie was using those mushrooms now, creating his own monster. Bacon *and* sausage patty (hey, he's the owner!), extra-sharp Cheddar, the beautiful wild mushrooms, white onion, jalapenos, and avocado. By the time Charlie added the sautéed mushrooms to his scramble, they had turned the color of smoked-salmon, or fingertips lit with a flashlight. The spots were amethyst and robin's-egg blue. Strange? Yes, but also very beautiful.

Charlie spooned his scramble onto an oval platter. The eggs took up a third of his plate. The other two thirds were taken up by the mushroom, potato, and bacon hash, along with raisin toast. He walked over to the table where he always sat when he made himself breakfast at his restaurant, placing his food down, before returning to the kitchen for a cup of coffee. Charlie came back, sat down and ate his breakfast.

His scramble was delicious! Charlie had really outdone himself this time, 'Praise Xushathula!', and the mushrooms!?

Charlie had cooked them to perfection; slightly crisp on the outside, a spongy meatiness when he bit into them. The mushrooms were extraordinary!

The taste...The texture?

Out of this world!

Thirty minutes after eating the mushrooms. Charlie burned with a fever that would have scorched the Devil himself. He was drenched in his own sweat. He shivers with a chill as if from the deepest sea.

Forty-five minutes after eating the mushrooms. Just as the mushroom had gone from a semi-transparent blue, to sickly yellow, to fleshy pink; so had Charlie turned from fleshy pink, to sickly yellow, to semi-transparent blue. Bright marigold and electric blue spots are now pulsating all over his skin; Charlie's flesh has become wiggly, like gelatin, the shadow of his skeleton visible beneath the skin…

An hour after eating the mushrooms. Gross, fungal growths, now cover Charlie Meyer's entire body. He is still mostly man-shaped. The growths are the strange fruits of cactus, or anemones from the ocean. The growths are pulsating gold and blue light. Charlie's flesh is as transparent as a pane of frosted glass. The Charlie-Thing dreams of deep space; riding an asteroid past whirling constellations; passing red dwarfs, crawling nebulas, and dying planets. The Charlie-Thing doesn't think in terms of time, so it's unknown how long it takes for the meteorite to travel to Earth…

An hour and fifteen minutes after eating the mushrooms. The Charlie-Thing remembers burning up, almost to nothing, when the meteorite entered Earth's atmosphere. The Charlie-Thing remembers being covered by cool soil, as the meteorite plunged into the dirt. Charlie Meyers' appendages that haven't grafted themselves to his now trunk-like body, have dropped to the ground, as if they were rotten vegetation. The appendages are covered in the beautiful mushrooms, along with the orange and blue fruiting bodies. The smell is that of a humid fungal infection; an over-ripe sweet along with a fermented sour. That last part of Charlie's brain can still recall the taste of the mushrooms...He remembers they were delicious...

An hour and a half after eating the mushrooms. Where Charlie's right arm has dropped and split open like a ripe zucchini, two more fruiting fungus stalks have sprouted up. A third stalk has sprung from Charlie's left leg, this one larger than the other two. The largest, the fourth stalk-thing, is the most terrible. It's as tall as a man. The Charlie-Thing remembers growing healthy, within the safe confines of Earth. How long had it been in the Earth, since Charlie had plucked its first growths? It didn't know why, but the thing thinks at least 10,000 years... The Charlie-Thing is a tube-like shape, spreading out into a mess of writhing chaos where it grows up from the floor. The fruiting bodies have hatched writhing tentacles, and sucker-mouths, with sharp, flickering tongues. Multiple eyes blink in unison, eyes placed in no rational pattern. The most horrible thing is that... Anyone who knew Charlie Meyers... They would know, and recognize, his face as the mask this monstrosity now wore! A mask hiding even more of the fleshy, writhing, lashing, and fruiting fungal growths blooming behind it. A mask hiding its hideous, ravenous mouth...

***

Four years after eating the mushrooms. Last week, a fence was completed around the building that was once El Cruz's most jumping breakfast joint. Breakfast being one of the seaside town's favorite past-times, over the last four years many a breakfast lover wondered, while staring at the boarded-up building; what had happened to shut down Occult Omelet? There was local gossip of some sort; A weird fungus invasion. Everyone figured it was black mold, which was pretty common for El Cruz. Last year the Health Department had entered the building, claiming it an ecological disaster site. The place was going to have to be torn down, razed with fire, and scrubbed clean with acid. First, there would have to be research done on the strange fungus that was found inside.

Government research. But, bureaucracy runs slowly. Until, one day, people driving plain white vans, wearing white haz-mat suits, decide to show up:

Translucent blue stalks, like giant cauliflowers, covered in mushrooms and fungal bark; four of them, equal in size, grow inside the Occult Omelet. A thin membrane with Swiss cheese holes, connects the four weird stalks. Besides mushrooms, the stalks are covered in pulsing growths of marigold orange, and electric blue; the fruit looks swollen and ripe. A sickly sweet smell of decay fills the entire space. The Charlie-Thing is startled out of its slumber. The Charlie-Thing lashes out with tendrils and tentacles, breaking away the protective face barrier of the people's isolation suits. It all happens so fast... The two members from the CDC team are hit point blank in the face with the spores of exploding fruit.

2 months later they're both dead. They'd died agonizing deaths. The last time anyone was in the building (2 months ago), the fungus thing took up three quarters of the interior space. Luckily, the Charlie-Thing was growing faster now. And luckily for the Charlie-Thing, bureaucracy still runs slowly...

At night, the fungus creature flexes and heaves; its bulk thrashing against the walls of the building that has become its cage. One night, soon, it will be able to splinter these wooden walls.

Not Tonight, or the night after that. Perhaps the following night, though. Definitely the night after that. It was strange how the fungus creature had come to consider time in human equations. And then, it remembered the taste of something delicious. Unfolding from the crenulations of one of the cauliflower-things heads, came tentacles and tendrils, pushing fourth a face; the mask of Charlie Meyers! The face was dwarfed by the monstrosity's massive bulk. The thing had always hidden that mask (writhing tentacles and whipping tendrils, too), when humans had entered its lair.

Until that time 2 months ago...

***

Tonight! Two sentient eyes open, in that parody of a human face; a face attached to an unbelievably ghastly thing. It was dreaming of riding the frozen meteorite just before it awoke; remembering that chill, the vacuum of deepest, darkest space. The eyes of the Charlie-Thing look through a small opening in a boarded-up window. It can feel the flexing and breaking of first dry-wall, and then lumber. It can see just a sliver of the ocean, off in the distance down the street. When it broke free of this cage, any minute now, it would go there. Something told the fungus thing that the water was cold and dark, like space. A different voice, of something slumbering deep in the Pacific, whispered in the Charlie-Thing's mind that it would thrive there; down in the ocean's freezing depths...

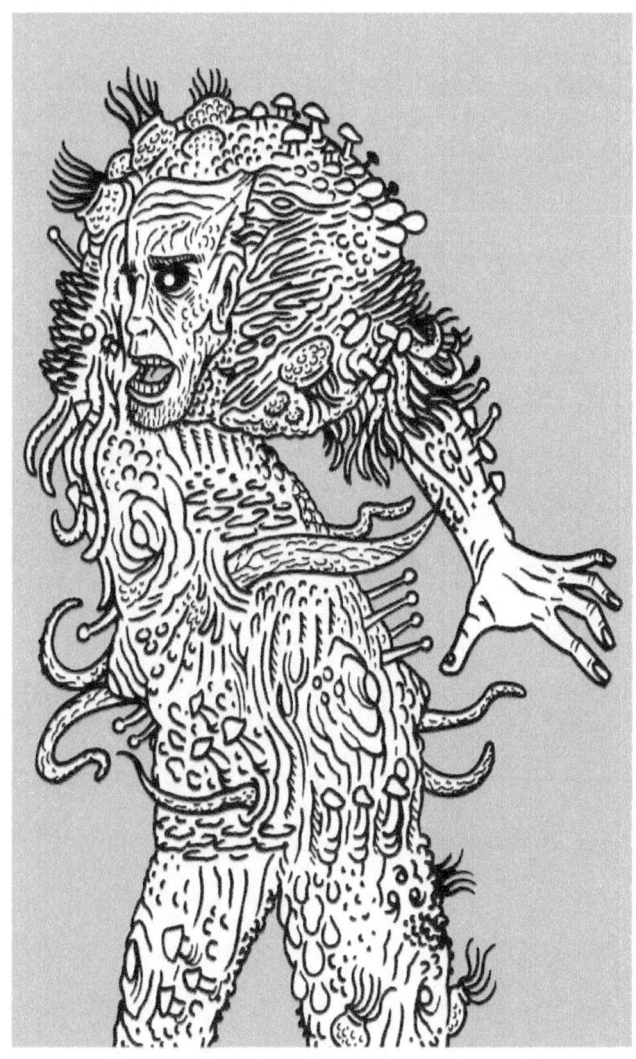

Hashbrown's Revenge

Tonight. Tonight's the night that things are going to change. Forever. Only two hours until the sun dropped off the edge of the world, plunging red-hot into the deep, dark cold of the Pacific Ocean. Then, the stars would rise. Align! In a constellation that hadn't been seen for thousands upon thousands of years! Wicked little stars, winking their evil little lights upon an unsuspecting world.

The place; Mid-Town, El Cruz, California. The man; Ashley Brown, but people called him Hashbrown.

Ashley Brown was the kind of guy that almost everyone in town knew. He'd grown up in the haunted seaside town of El Cruz. He was born there, and, he would most likely die there.

'They'll all die here!' Ash Brown thought.

Back when Ashley was in kindergarten, El Cruz was a much smaller place. That was 1965. It was also the year that had slowly driven Ashley Brown to this very moment. That kindergarten year, Ash had eaten a spoiled shrimp-salad sandwich from the El Cruz Seaside Diner, shitting his shorts in class the very next morning. Some smart-ass kindergartener had yelled out that the shit-stain looked like hash-browns on his butt. So from that day fourth, Ash Brown, became forever known as Hashbrown; the kid who had shit his shorts...

"God-Damn that fuckin' El Cruz Seaside Diner! I loved that shrimp-salad sandwich," Hashbrown would lament, talking to no one in particular. No. Ashley Brown. Tonight he would become *Ashley* Brown once more. *Never* Hashbrown! Not *ever* again. Tonight *Hashbrown* would be cast off forever!

Life had been tough for poor old Ashley. What he lacked in good looks, he made up for by being smart. *Book* smart. Ashley Brown didn't do too well in school, though, being prone to daydreams and fantasizing, his teachers had said. But boy, could that kid read. Ash Brown was *too* smart; found out the hard way, that *no one* likes a smarty pants. Especially one who'd had a hash-brown in them. All through elementary school, and then all through junior high, Hashbrown was ridiculed; made the butt of almost every mean spirited prank. So Ash Brown retreated from reality, delving deeper into fiction. Science fiction. Then, eventually, weird fiction...

Instead of skateboarding, surfing, playing in bands, and chasing girls, Ash Brown spent his high school years reading. At that point, he'd gravitated towards some pretty heavy stuff; history; magic; religion; witchcraft; demonology. As his interests grew darker, Ashley began attempting certain rituals; certain *rites*. His junior year, when Hashbrown was seventeen, He would forever swear that he'd called something up. Something that he shouldn't have... Something that that he couldn't put back down.

The following day, at El Cruz High School, during gym class, Ash saw the terrible shadow of some horrible thing crawl across the gymnasium floor. He'd been scared shitless. Again. In front of the entire co-ed third period gym class. For the second time in twelve years, Hashbrown had shit his shorts.

When Hashbrown was seventeen he had been diagnosed with schizophrenia...

Two people came strolling out of the El Cruz Seaside Diner, which was located 12 blocks from the ocean. There *is* an ocean view of sorts, though; A mural of El Cruz, captured in all its mid-summer, late afternoon glory. Complete with amusement park, lighthouse, shredding surfers, and mermaids! It was like being at a crowded, dirty beach while drowning in the shallows.

The couple quickly approached Hashbrown; an elderly gentleman who looked like a bloated sperm whale, arm in arm with a desiccated mummy of an old woman, wearing perfume that smelled like a dead flower arrangement.

"That shrimp-salad sandwich always hits the spot," Moby Dick wheezed, squeezing out a gurgling fart.

"More like two fucking shrimp-salad sandwiches, you pig!" the mummy cursed. "Along with a bowl of God-damn chowder, garlic toast, a dinner salad *drowned* in ranch dressing, fucking *french*-fries, a strawberry milkshake, fucking hot apple pie—*a la mode*—and three bites of my God-damn Devil's Food cake!"

"Yeah, but I had a diet Coke," The white whale squelched, before blowing more fetid air from his puckering blowhole. He followed up with a booming belch, satisfaction and pride creeping over his face.

"I hope you wore your fucking diapers?" The mummy's voice was as grating as the sands of Egypt. What a magnificent beast the whale must be, to endure such a blistering sandstorm...

"Excuse me?" Ash politely asked, greeting the elderly couple at the bottom of the handicap ramp, which had been dressed up to resemble a pier. Right down to barnacles, clams and starfish. There was even a pelican. "Would you happen to have any spare change?"

"There's no such fuckin' thing! FUCKIN' BEAT IT, YA CREEP!!!" The fat, sperm whale of a man, bellowed; his face turning from pale white to a glowing rose red. Globules of spittle hit Hashbrown in the face. Due to all the exertion, Moby Dick squeezed yet more raunchy air from his flabby butt cheeks...

Hashbrown stood there with a thousand-mile stare; whale slobber on his face; whale flatulence filling his nostrils... the whale's wind was the smell of some bloated dead thing rotting on a beach—

"Raymond! You calm down—Buzzzzzzz—what your doctor said? That you—Buzzzzzzzzzzzz—or else your temper is fucking—Buzzzzzzzzzzzzzzzzzz—you a fucking heart attack! You need to calm—

Buzzzzzzzzzzzzzzzzzzzzzzzzzzzzzzzzzzzzzzzzzzzzzzzzzz"

Eventually, Hashbrown only heard buzzing.

He was rabid.

He was a madman.

At that moment, Hashbrown was every dog who's ever been kicked. Every soldier who had ever fought the good fight, only to be disrespected and spit on upon his arrival home. Hashbrown, opening up a verbal salvo that would've made someone with Tourette's syndrome proud, barked:

"FUCKIN'-COCK-EATIN' DICK-FACE! I ATE A SHIT-COVERED SHRIMP-CUNT-SALAD-SANDWICH and I POO'D MY FUCKIN' SHORTS! FUCKIN' POOPED MY FUCKING SHORTS!! I POO'D—IN MY FUCKIN' SHORTS—WHEN I WAS JUST A FUCKIN' TINY LITTLE FUCKIN' *ASSHOLE* KID!!! SHIT MY SHORTS IN FRONT OF THE WHOLE FUCKIN' *ASSHOLE* CLASS!" Hashbrown manically screamed, *his* spit now pelting the *whale's* face. "SO GO FUCK YOUR WIFE'S MUMMIFIED SLIT YOU FAT FUCKIN' WHALE!!! EL CRUZ SEASIDE DINER RUINED LIFE!! RUINED MY ENTIRE LIFE...*RUINED* IT BY PUTTING A SHITTY HASHBROWN, RHYMES WITH ASH BROWN,

POO-POO STAIN IN MY FUCKIN' SHORTS! AND YOU CAN'T BE BOTHERED FOR A FEW FUCKIN' MEASLY FUCKIN' CENTS?!!!"

The manager of the diner came hustling through the front door, jogging down the ramp to confront Hashbrown, "Mister Brown?! Have you stopped taking your medications, Mister Brown?! I've called the police, and they're sending an officer as we speak!" The weasel-faced man lied, hollering through his yellow nicotine-stained teeth.

Hashbrown looked around, noticing all the attention he'd garnered. Besides Moby Dick and the Mummy, there were another dozen or so people gathered in a crescent moon shape, surrounding him like a pack of wolves. Hashbrown despised the police. Trying to tell him where he could sleep; telling him where he could stand. Then the fear set in. Hashbrown had been on the receiving end of a few baton-beat-downs in his day! He began to panic, bolting off through a hole in the crowd. As Hashbrown went darting down towards the direction of the sea, he heard a voice rise above the crowd; a voice that was harsh, and full of ridicule...

"HEY! I used to go to *school* with that guy! They used to call him Hashbrown, 'cause he took a shit in his *shorts,* and the shit-stain looked like a *hash*-brown!"

***

By the time Hashbrown had turned 21, He was living on Squid Row; El Cruz's version of Skid Row. Four square blocks of corrugated metal buildings alongside weather beaten wooden shacks, surrounded by hurricane fences. There were a few old Victorian houses sprinkled about, all but one of them fallen so far into decay, that they've become charming, in their own haunted, dilapidated way. Nestled in along the decrepit waterfront are a handful of trendy restaurants, taking advantage of the areas abundant fish markets. The fishmongers keep the place pretty safe until five o'clock; the restaurants keep it sort-of safe until midnight...

Although, on some foggy autumn nights, when there were no takers at the eateries; even around seven o'clock? Or, when the lights of the El Cruz Beach Boardwalk are never turned on at all, being the off-season, and all? Those times at three in the morning, on certain nights, when certain stars align just right? Those are all good times to steer clear of Squid Row.

Most people who grew up in El Cruz avoided the place after dark. Like the Bubonic Plague; Or these days, it would be Ebola, I guess...

Countless waitresses, getting off work late at night, along with numerous college students trying to purchase their drug of choice, or super-creeps trying to pick up a working girl; They would all tell the same sort of stories. Stories about weird people they would see wandering the waterfront of Squid Row. Especially on the foggy nights. Now, sure, most of those people were just plain old, bat-shit crazy. For El Cruz, homeless population 2000, I'm talking about your run-of-the-mill homeless person. But those other ten percent that respectable-citizen-type people see? The things *they* tell stories about? There's nothing run-of-the-mill about them.

They're described as looking amphibian, but, with human traits; never human with amphibian traits, It's always amphibian with human traits. These creatures have large, bulging, luminescent eyes, with flat noses and huge nostrils; with the sharp teeth of a sand shark. These hulking creatures almost always appeared to be dragging some kind of bulky weight at their backs. People describe catching glimpses of things resembling fish tails, wiggling and slapping along the concrete behind them. These tails weren't the only thing fishy about them, either. Their smell was fearsome; a noxious combination of spoiled seafood, decomposing kelp, along with the aroma of beached whale; always wafting an all-encompassing briny-ness. One creature in particular has been sighted more frequently than the others. This is one description of that creature:

"...the thing looked like an enormous bull-frog. At least its face did. It had broad shoulders and a slim waist, like a swimmer. Whatever it was it had a massive barrel-chest. Its arms and legs were long a skinny, but

you could see muscles bulging beneath fabric. Which brings us to the strangest part. The thing was dressed like a fisherman. Or a longshoreman, maybe? Did I mention it had a tail... like a fish? And the smell of the thing was beyond awful. Anyone who's ever smelled spoiled fish would know what I'm talking about..."

There were plenty of sightings like that on foggy nights, during the off-season, along the waterfront of El Cruz's Squid Row...

Hashbrown ran through the little rat's warren that was Squid Row, all the way down to the waterfront, then out and on to one of the small fishing piers. He stopped, looking up the beach to the myriad twinkling lights of the El Cruz Beach Boardwalk. It was not the off-season; it was, in fact, a hot August night. Not quite night... it was more like dusk. The clatter of the rides along with the screams of their riders rode upon the zephyr's breeze, eventually reaching Hashbrown's ears. The first few stars began to twinkle in the purple haze overhead. It was a glorious evening...

Evening?

Didn't Hashbrown have something to do this evening? No. Not Hashbrown; he was going to become Ashley Brown. *Ash*ley Brown, the most terrifying wizard the modern world had ever known! Down on the pier, Ashley Brown craned his head towards the sky, nodding. Again the screams of thrill seekers, the sounds of amusement park rides, cut through the air. 'Fuck them all! They all die tonight!' He thought.

"Yes! The stars rise in their proper houses! They are right! The stars are *right!*" his voice cackled with glee. A voice that hadn't known glee for a very, very long time. A sound so foreign to Ashley Brown's ears, that he startled himself. His brow furrowed.

Tonight, Ash Brown would pay his debt to the Thing that he'd called up all those years before. After all, the Thing had saved his life, as wretched as his life had been. Ash Brown had finally kneeled before that presence, five years ago; the night of his birthday. He'd been a boozed up, drugged-out addict, with both feet in the grave. Ash Brown had died that night; stopped breathing for thirty-three minutes, after smoking a hit of crack cocaine. That was how long it took for the first responders to show up on the scene. For some reason, they always took a long time getting down to Squid Row. Same with the Police. And the Fire Department. Weird, huh?

Anyways; when the paramedics arrived, they'd decided to shock old Ash Brown, Hashbrown, just for the hell of it. Call it a sort of fiftieth birthday present. Even though they were 99.9% sure that the dude was as dead as a Thanksgiving Day turkey. To the paramedics' surprise, Hashbrown's eyes popped open, rolling completely back into his head; two orbs of pure white. Then, the crazy old coot began speaking some strange, guttural language, "Like he was speakin' in tongues!", one drunken old hobo who'd witnessed it would declare. Another old wino had commented on Hashbrown's eyes, glowing with a blue witch-fire. The first responders had pat each other on the back, in a congratulatory fashion that night, for saving old Hashbrown's life...

Ashley Brown knew better. It was the Thing he'd called up, when he was 17, that had brought him back to the land of the living. In the throes of death, in the darkest place Hashbrown had ever been, the Thing promised him life; then power beyond imagination, *if,* and only if, Ash could open the portal of the prison holding it beneath the entire weight of the Pacific Ocean; On a night when the stars were right. The Thing had promised Ash Brown he wouldn't shit his shorts before coming to, on that now distant night of his fiftieth birthday. An act that had forever won Ash Brown's devotion and gratitude. For *that*, he would be eternally grateful to the Thing he'd called up—

Tonight was that night. He must speak the words, unbroken. It was the Thing that had told him about the little forbidden black book that Ash now had in his possession...

Ash Brown pulled a small, worn book, which could have been mistaken for a bible, from the waistband of his dirty turquoise sweatpants. His once bright yellow t-shirt had faded to the dull, grim color of rotten teeth. Like his sweatpants, it was also filthy dirty. A small swarm of flies formed a halo about his head.

The book was definitely *not* a bible. He opened the cracked leather cover of the ancient tome, flipping through dozens of musty old pages, thumbing quickly past vile illustrated pages. For this book contained such horrific things—

The sky was turning from violet, to a deeper, royal purple. Stars began popping through the fabric of the evening sky. A weird blue fog began stirring on the horizon. The Pacific sloshed gently against the pilings of the pier, the shrill cry of a gull drifting down from somewhere overhead. The planks of the pier creaked, swaying in time with the small, but surging, swell of the sea.

Soon. The time would be so soon...

Hashbrown; No! Ashley Brown would read from the blasphemous book he had stolen from the El Cruz Public Library, awakening the Thing waiting beneath the sea. It was so far away, but oh, how sound can travel underwater...

He stopped at a page in the stinky old book.

Ashley Brown began reading, unholy words that would correct the path; the words that would change his destiny. The words that would obliterate his past...

"Oh Glorious One! That which can pass through the portal, tonight, while the stars are right," Ash Brown was not speaking English. Or any other language known to humankind, for that matter. The language he spoke had been dead for 50,000 years. "Oh, Greatest of the Seven Queens, who slumbers in the depths of the vast Pacific Ocean... She who shall rise from her watery prison of H'fuu'Aru, this very night!

"Hear the voice of a believer; hear my praises. It is I who will release your Highness! Rise from your volcanic depths! Rattle the entire Earth with your awakening!" On cue, the ground along the waterfront began to quake. "As tribute I offer you this town, nothing more than a morsel, for an appetite as great as yours. They are almost not even worthy, but there are many places such as this. And you must be hungry. There are places worthy of your regal hunger, though! All the great cities of Man! In fact, there's an entire world!" Ash Brown was channeling the high priests of Hyboria.

"For only a Queen of your stature and breeding, can give birth to a hive. It has been written in the forbidden books, that once upon a time, two million years ago, your hive ruled the entire planet. It has been written that it shall be so, once again..."

A handful of people passing by along the waterfront, shocked by the earthquake, began gathering at the entrance of the pier from which Hashbrown was delivering his harsh alien liturgy. Hashbrown was violently yelling the weird language at the top of his lungs. While still reciting the invocation, Ash brown noticed a man pull a cellphone from his pocket, dial it, and raise it to his ear. It didn't matter. Hashbrown was too far along...too far gone...one more passage to go...

Unbroken—

"Xushathula! Seventh and mightiest Queen of the Rim of Fire! I break the portal of your prison. I break the chains that bind you, in the depths of H'fuu'Aru. I've aligned the stars for your coming! I have done this in devotion to you. I have done this for Your Majesty. Tonight, I ask for your awakening! Your…" Hashbrown's voice was no longer even his voice. His eyes were burning pits of glowing blue light… Waves began rising from the sea—Then!

Another rolling quake!

"Hey! It's Hashbrown! Ash Brown, Ash Brown, shit his shorts, it's Hashbrown!" It was the man from the diner; it was the smart-ass kindergartener from 1965; it was anyone and everyone who'd ever called him Hashbrown. One by one, the group began chiming in.

"Your," Hashbrown stumbled and stopped for a brief moment. Hardly a second.

The crowds' chanting swept away his train of thought, "Ash Brown, Ash Brown, shit his shorts it's Hashbrown!"

Time is now—

All Hashbrown had to say was, "time is now", in whatever alien language he'd bee channeling. Three small words. It was already too late, though. He'd paused…just…long…enough…

So, instead of the greater glory of raising some ancient and terrible god-thing from its millennia's long doze, this was Hashbrown's revenge; his voice rising over the hollow thunder of the building surf:

"Oh…why you dirty, no good Mother-fuckin'-cock-suckin' two-balled-bitches! You're all a bunch of creeps, that can lick my stinking brown shit-hole, you

God-damn ass-faces! Cock fuck shit ass," Hashbrown shrieked; in English; with no small amount of conviction. Tourette's-O-Mania!

Hashbrown had read enough from the book to open a temporary portal; the manifestation of the Thing merely an ectoplasmic projection of the cursed goddess, which laid imprisoned beneath the sea. It was only one limb of the thousand limbed deity, but such things are still not without their power....

There was a massive boom, followed by a sound wave that blew out most of the windows, all up and down the entire waterfront; the blast knocking even the hardiest onlookers off their feet and to the ground. Of the three people that claimed to have witnessed what had happened to Ashley Brown, only one of them could be persuaded to talk about what he'd seen.

The following, for your consideration, is the account given by local commercial fisherman, from the up-standing El Cruz Gilman Family, Drew Gilman:

"After the sound wave blew me over, I quickly scrambled around into a crouching position. Now understand, I only caught a glimpse, but I don't think my mind could've taken any more than that glimpse. I noticed this boiling blue light...way, way out in the ocean... Where it was glowing, the water was bubbling like a hot pot of water. And, oh my God, the Thing coming out of that boiling cauldron of seawater!? Some sort of... tentacle? Made from that same weird blue light glowing out in the sea, like a ghost. Or jellyfish,

maybe? Where there would've been suckers on an octopus, this thing had ferocious faces! Blinking, glowing eyes...Bright, green eyes! Horrible, gnashing, savage teeth! And the size of the God-damned Thing! Those faces were much larger than human faces! Twice the size... They weren't human, either. The tentacle was as thick around as an elephant's chest! Maybe even thicker! Nothing in nature could...or should, be that big. The whole Thing was covered along its dorsal side in quills, spines, tendrils, tentacles and weird grasping... uh... appendages? Yeah, I guess they'd have to be called appendages. The Thing had grabbed that poor homeless guy; Boy oh boy, he was cursin' up a storm, he was! I'd given him my spare change on several different occasions. I always felt sorry for the guy. I'd seen him around El Cruz for years. I'd always heard people call him Hashbrown, you know, to rile him up. Until that—whatever that... nightmare thing was— carried him off to those bubbling blue lights in the ocean, I never knew his real name. Now I'll never forget it. As the Thing pulled him out to sea the last thing he was screaming, between bursts of mad laughter, over and over, was, 'My name is Ashley Brown!'"

The
MARSHVILLE
CARNECERIA

Marshville Carneceria
Burrito de Deseyunos:
Hueveos, Largo de Cerdo,
Queso, Potatoes & Salsa
Mantar Frigo!
Keep Refigerated!
24oz.

Crispy Bacon

The following is a newspaper clipping from the El Cruz Inquisitor...

The Ramirez brothers of Marshville have run an extremely successful eatery for the last 30 years, since the brothers took the business over from their father and uncle. The Marshville Carneceria has passed through 5 generations of Ramirez brothers. Even since the early days of Marshville, The Carneceria, has been a fixture of the community for our neighbors to the south. This reporter regrets to say that she has eaten at The Carneceria on many occasions, while out on assignment. I've just regurgitated thinking about how many times... anyone else who has ever eaten at the popular eatery is bound to do the same after reading this article.

First, a brief history of the Ramirez Family...

The Original Ramirez brothers came to California in 1775. They were Conquistadors riding along to protect Father Julio Serrano; as we'll see, Father Serrano was an extremely eccentric man. From

1775 to 1783, the Ramirez brothers assisted Father Serrano in establishing not 1, but 3 Missions on California's central coast. A remarkable feat, even by modern standards, these strange Missions were built in Pescadero, El Cruz, and Point Prieta.

Three years after the Missions had been erected? They were disowned and disavowed by the Catholic Church. In a letter from a missionary of that period, to the Vatican, Father Garcia writes (translated from Latin):

"...and the geometry of the place seems off-kilter, it is hard to describe in what way exactly, although the proportions seem to create an uneasy feeling in my very core. As if I had consumed too much wine the night before, though I'd drunk no more than a small glass, so that the blood of the Christ would give me the strength needed to bear witness to the last of these 3 abominations of the Faith! To dare call them Missions of God? I have seen with my own two eyes the —strangeness—of that place in Pescadero, and then the even stranger one at El Cruz. This last place at Point Prieta is by far the worst, the last of the three that Serrano and his men built. It is rumored that things other than men have had a—hand—in erecting these sites. At first everything appears to be normal, until closer inspection of statuary, the things in the stained glass, the details of the artworks, not to mention the Stations of the Cross...My God! What I thought to be a statue not unlike Leonardo's, of the virgin mother cradling our savior? Her eyes were too far apart, and her pained smile seemed to be filled with the fangs of a feral animal.

What I mistook as our Lord and Savior, was an eyeless creature; tentacles of an octopus, though by the dozens, crowned its head like hair. The eyes that should have been in the things face were carved in the stigmata wounds of the crucifixion. It was covered in fine relief scales from head to toe. I shudder to think of it and I shall say the Lord's Prayer as soon as this letter is finished. As shall I take a draught of the blood of Christ, only to help me sleep through the night, or perhaps..."

The letter ends abruptly. Two interesting side notes; first, Father Garcia went missing shortly after the letter had been sent to the Vatican, and Serrano was excommunicated from the church; second, the Mission at Point Prieta was burned down by a group of Native American guides who had been escorting Father Garcia on his California trek, along with two "outlaws" from the area that would eventually become San Francisco...

And it was the 1906 earthquake that brought down the Mission at Pescadero. Another interesting side note; Pescadero lies approximately 35 miles of San Francisco, and some geologists debate the epicenter being Pescadero, and *not* San Francisco. The day of the 1906 earthquake, there were a number of curious sightings. Many people from different vantage points along the coast, report seeing something, "the size of a small mountain", rise out of the sea at Pescadero; people reported seeing weird nebulous clouds, what some referred to as "tendril's of mist", make their way to shore towards the Old Mission. It wasn't until the mountainous mass dropped back *into* the Pacific Ocean that the historic earthquake rocked the California coast. At least, according to some old timers.

And just what happened to the Ramirez Brothers, you may ask?

In 1795, nearly a decade after the dust had settled around their involvement with the infamous Padre Serrano, and the mysterious whisperings of how the Missions were really completed in such a short amount of time, the Ramirez brothers settled down in Marshville. That same year, Esteban and Antonio established The Carneceria, or El Carneceria, as it was known in those days. That same rundown wooden building with the charming, peeled white paint, that's always been down on Old Marsh Drive. Though the Carneceria sells chicken and beef, it's the original Ramirez brothers' recipe for cooking pig that has had people turning out in droves for their succulent pork tacos. Pork tacos that it seems have *always* been to die for. The old family recipe passed down from 1795 has never changed, a tradition that has remained intact. Ingredients so simple, yet so delicious; Or, so I used to think… A freshly made corn tortilla, soft and warm, piled high with that tender pork. But don't call it carnitas! The Ramirez brothers call it Largo de Cerdo. The roasted meat is chopped to strands, by one of the smiling brothers, hacking away at the pork with expert strikes of a cleaver. The Largo de Cerdo is topped with cilantro, white onion, and a splash of a fiery red salsa; some patrons began calling the salsa 'Satan's Kiss', for the burning sensation that it could cause. Let's just say it was a real pain in the rear! But people loved it, and there has been a line around that building since I was a little girl.

Thankfully those days are over. The smell of crispy bacon, of Largo de Cerdo, has come to an end.

It was that *very* dish; that *treasured* family recipe; that *filthy* dirty secret that caused the El Cruz Sheriff's department to storm the charming old building, down on Old Marsh Road. Both of the Ramirez brothers were apprehended without incident. For anyone who has ever eaten at The Marshville Carneceria, I'm very sorry to report that the secret Ramirez family recipe isn't such a secret anymore. Largo de Cerdo, roughly translates to Long Pork. Anyone aware of maritime disasters will recognize the term. Long Pork is human flesh…

I've just returned to typing, after a fit of gagging and retching, thinking about licking the grease of that delicious, succulent meat from my fingers. Even as my stomach churns I have a craving for those tacos. This reporter is both nauseous *and* hungry.

And No! I'm not pregnant!

Anyhow, once the Ramirez brothers were in law enforcement's custody, they sang like canaries; answered any question the authorities wanted to know. Only their answers were more like pleas of insanity. Both men's accounts were nearly identical. To avoid repetition, I will relate the rantings and ravings of Esteban. This is how so many unsuspecting people on the central coast, came to unknowingly commit the vilest of taboos—Oh, Lord please, oh please, forgive us—Cannibalism!

This is the statement of Esteban Ramirez:

"The Ramirez family learned many things in our service to Padre Serrano, while overseeing the construction of those magnificent Missions, each one built to represent a God that most men could never hope to understand… Then again that is the ways of gods, is it not? Well, the blessed Padre Serrano showed us things that only a handful of other initiates have been allowed to see. The Ramirez family have been knights as far back as we can trace our heritage. Since the times of the Templars, we learned to disguise our gods as angels and saints of the Catholic Church; to hide our rites and rituals within the church's own. But we've always served—others—in the guise of the Christian faith! As did Padre Serrano. It was other servants of our gods, similar yet different than men, that helped build the Mission at Pescadero. Padre Serrano, using an ancient spell, would summon rainclouds at dusk, calling down localized rain storms. He would do this several times a month. On those nights, an army numbering in the hundreds would come from the sea. This horde of creatures would set to work, completing amounts of work in one night, that would have taken human men in the same number, at least a month to complete. And then, an hour before sunrise, the creatures would shamble back down to the shore, and disappear into the ocean… the creatures could only work in the rain, and they shunned the light of day.

"Padre Serrano knew of these Deep Ones, as he referred to them. Although the Ramirez family had always believed in the Eldest Secrets, as our faith is known, none from our line had ever seen proof of our faith, until the blessed Padre Serrano summoned those majestic creatures from the depths, walking from the waves, of the mighty Pacific Ocean! Padre Serrano had a way of finding special places, you see? Places where the fabric between the spaces is thin. Understand? And so it was with El Cruz, and Point Prieta. It was at El Cruz that we learned our recipe for Largo de Cerdo...

"In those days, the entire area was known as the Valley of the Shunned. The inhabitants were a lost tribe; strangely pale of skin, with blue or green eyes, their hair predominantly red. These people were large in all ways imaginable and very attractive. They knew no shame, preferring to wear only the skin they had been born in. They were all tattoo'd in bold, black slashing shapes upon arms, legs and ribcages. Each member of the tribe wore one piece of jewelry, made from a fascinating metal, the color a swirling iridescence of purples, magentas, and blues swimming in gold. This exquisite metal was artistically fashioned into necklaces, bracelets, armbands, and ankle bracelets, all carved with creatures of such a fantastic nature. Other than the jewelry, the tribe members all wore a simple belt made of some sort of leather. The belt buckles, so finely carved, could have been eye-sockets whittled out of a human skull. Attached to these belts were various leather pouches, each member of the tribe wore a knife at their sides, the handles carved from what seemed to have been a human thigh-bone. When Padre Serrano's party found the valley, we saw those knives put to use for the first time. In an instant, several of our scouts fell beneath the stabbing blades of these giant, pale, tattoo'd redheaded savages. Within ten minutes the lost tribe had slaughtered all but 3 members of Padre Serrano's party. The Ramirez brothers, thanks to armor, and skill with both spear and sword. And Serrano himself, due to dark sorceries. The tribe was awe-struck at the ability to withstand their onslaught, and as such, raised Serrano to the level of priest-king, and saw the Ramirez brothers as his divine protectors. Heroes, of sorts.

"All through the night of the slaughter, and again through the next rotation of sun and moon, the tribe worked. 36 hours straight, in teams of two, a man and a woman would work together butchering the dead members of Padre Serrano's party, occasionally stopping for brief moments of intercourse, before setting back to working on a corpse with those terrible knives. Next came the preparation of the meats. All but 3 of the 25 butchered men were placed in crudely made carts. The carts were tethered to large smoke grey goats, with eyes the color of a harvest moon. Two dozen of them, in all.

"The 3 cadavers that had been set aside for us, were the smallest men in Serrano's party. Juan's torso had been cleaved open at the sternum, cracked wide and slathered with salt from the sea, then placed on blocks above a fire-pit. His head had been removed, his mouth stuffed with a mixture of minced organs, onions, cilantro, corn and testicles. This was roasted in a clay oven. There were sausages of ground up innards, and bone split to reveal rich marrow. Other things that looked like sausages but were not, if you understand. These the women ate. The arms and legs were very carefully stripped of their flesh, revealing the source of the lost tribe's leather used for their belts. Rich sauces were made with combinations of root vegetables, herbs, blood and stomach enzymes cooked to a boil.

"The bodies of Gonzalvo and Javier were prepared in similar, yet, slightly different ways. Except for their heads. Their heads were placed in the goat drawn wagons…

"At the tribes' feast, the head of Juan, skin crackling and sizzling, was served on a large wooden platter to Padre Serrano. Mouth, nostrils and eye-sockets steaming fragrant white smoke. This was the tribe bestowing their new priest-king with the choicest cuts, usually reserved only for their god. Brains and ball sacks.

"In other words, a very great honor, no?

"And the Ramirez brothers?

"We were fed the food of the lost tribe's warrior elite, the rump roast, prepared in the manner of the Largo de Cerdo taco, that we still proudly serve today. I don't need to tell you, officer's…if I'm not mistaken you guys were regulars. Delicious, huh? Anyway…

"The tribe watched on in anticipation. There had been other guests served up this holiest of meals in times past. To dine was to worship with The One-Under-The-Hill; to decline was to feed The One-Under-The-Hill. So far, no dinner guest the tribe had ever had made the decision to dine upon the feast, placed before them…

"The lost tribe had no way of knowing that the three of us, Padre Serrano, my brother Antonio and I, had already passed a similar test with the Deep Ones, at the Mission de Pescadero. They enjoyed the taste of human flesh, and made it known that we must eat it, too. At least the tribe preferred their meat cooked, you know?

"The tribe collectively held their breath, as Padre Serrano plucked a large chunk of meat from Juan's cheek, ripping it away from the smoking skull, and raised it high, as if making an offering. Serrano brought the roasted flesh to his nostrils, inhaling. Then he took a giant bite, gulping it down to the uproarious cheers of the lost tribe. This was followed by another mouthful, and another. Fistful after fistful, of Padre Serrano's manservant's face flesh, until there was nothing but grinning skull staring through strands of ravaged meat.

"The tribe's attention turned to Antonio, and me. We each tucked into our platters of Largo de Cerdo to the hearty applause and whooping of the tribe. After, the entire tribe joined in, feasting on the meat provided by Juan, Gonzalvo, and Javier.

"After the meal, we were shown carvings in stone. A great bas-relief, of The One-Under-The-Hill. Being initiates of the Elder Secrets, Padre Serrano, Antonio and I recognized their One-Under-The-Hill as one of the demi-gods of our own faith. I won't say his true name. Through a makeshift form of sign language, the chieftain of the tribe informed us that the following night, we would go with the chosen to give an offering to The One-Under-The-Hill. After that, the night descended into a ritualistic orgy, in which we were invited to join. It was only the first of many nights that we celebrated in such a feral manner, during our time spent with The Shunned! That was the name the tribe had given to themselves, centuries ago.

"It was The Shunned who helped build the Mission de El Cruz. But on the nights of the full moon, for six consecutive months, The One-Under-The-Hill would come fourth and assist in the heaviest of lifting, which would seem to be of little to no effort for the behemoth creature. And each time we called forth the demi-god, we would raid a nearby settlement in the dead of night. The giant members of The Shunned making off with 2 people apiece, slung over their shoulders like sacks of grain, to appease the terrible beast that lived under the hill. And a few for the tribe, of course. The demi-god is still, to this day, the most powerful entity I've ever witnessed with my own two eyes. I wasn't as involved with the building of the Mission de Point Prieta. Antonio accidently caught a glimpse out of the corner of his eye, of the god that was summoned to erect the majority of the building in one night, there. Antonio has been blind in that eye ever since. He wouldn't trade his eyesight for that briefest of glimpses, though, and he holds it over my head all the time. He'd seen a god, and lived to tell about it.

"Well, things eventually turned sour. The Vatican began sending men to investigate these 3 new churches, built in an incredibly short amount of time. It was the concern of the Holy See that these Missions erected so quickly, couldn't possibly convey the beauty and majesty that the Lord and savior Jesus Christ, so surely deserved (Here Esteban spit upon the floor of his holding cell). The first seven committees sent from the

Vatican became meals for these deities of our faith, the Gods of the Elder Secrets…

"Serrano, and my brother Antonio, killed Padre Renaldo Garcia, the night before he was to leave the Mission de Point Prieta. But, Garcia had told his scouts, should anything happen to him, they were to burn the Mission to the ground. And so they did. He'd secreted a letter to one of his men, one of the "outlaws" from Frisco. He escaped, and that letter was sent to the Vatican. That sent everything we'd worked towards into a downward spiral, man.

"After narrowly escaping the wrath of Vatican soldiers, Antonio and I set up our place in Marshville. That would've been back in '95. Eventually, a stagecoach run was set up, between San Francisco to the Mission de San Juan Batista. Before the days of the telephone, and, I'm talking landline—forget about cell phones—can you imagine, how many thousands of people went missing along that route, between 1849 'til 1920? Because *I* can. We were always careful, though. The stagecoaches would stop for a bite to eat, everyone had heard about our pork tacos and wanted to try them. We became very rich, very fast, with El Carneceria being supplemented by the plunder of highway robbery.

"Even since the days that El Carneceria opened its doors to the public, we've sent everything but the rump roasts north to El Cruz, as a weekly offering to The-One-Under-The-Hill. In the hills above El Cruz, descendants of The Shunned still live there. Lompico. Felton. Zeyantee. Some almost human, others the spawn of ungodly orgies! Padre Serrano, my brother Antonio, and I, are all partially responsible for spawning some of them ourselves. We still practice the old ways, every once in a great while. But we can wait, for the stars are almost right (here, subject smiles with a faraway look).

"The followers of the Elder Secrets practice, what the ignorant would perceive as black magic. Thanks to the guidance of Padre Serrano, Antonio and I, are now each of us powerful brujos. Sorcerers. We have sustained ourselves on human flesh for over 250 years. And we can live for another 250 years without ever eating or drinking again! Do you think you'll keep us trapped in a little cell? We who've nurtured the ideas of our faith for centuries?" (Interview concludes with Mr. Ramirez descending into maniacal laughter)

Esteban, who appears to be a man in his mid-forties, claims to in fact, be 333 years old. His brother Antonio claims to be 327. Both men will be seeing the inside of a mental institution for a very long time. One last interesting side note; when authorities searched the men's homes, known locally as Spanish Castle 1 and Spanish Castle 2, law enforcement found some interesting things. In each place, investigators found: An extremely sharp knife carved from a human femur, its handle covered in esoteric carvings; Libraries of books, some of which were believed to be fictional, all bound in bizarre leathers; And last, in each residence, an authentic suit of Spanish Conquistador's armor, complete with weapons and helm.

Both men are being held without bail while awaiting their trials...

Strong Coffee

The following pages were retrieved from the Journal of Max Whately, at his residence, by the EL Cruz Police Department. The case has yet to be solved, finding its way on to the E.C.P.D's ever growing list of "Mystery Files". Continue reading to draw your own conclusions:

riday, October 17- When I got back to the bungalow, from my super-strange bicycle ride down on the levy, I was still in a daze; in shock, really. I'd wheeled my trusty Schwinn into the garden shed (even though I don't remember doing that), before stumbling inside. I really snapped back to reality once I'd reached the safety of The Shack. After back to back to back bong-rips, I wrote the whole story down. My mind finally turned away from Gog, and had begun whining about not getting its morning coffee fix...

So, I'd dumped some coffee beans, 'Major Dicks' (delicious coffee... suckin' name!), from Pete's Coffee House, into my coffee grinder.

Whiiiiizzzzzzzzzzzzzzzzzz...zzzzzzzzzzz...zzzzzzz... zzzzzzzzzzz...

The coffee grinder whirred faster and faster. 13... 14... 15... The grinder screamed away, singing a banshee's wail. At the very height of its crescendo, the noise felt like audible icepicks, stabbing into my eardrums... 16... 17... *and*...18.

I'd scooped six heaping tablespoons out of the grinder into an unbleached paper filter, placing the filter into the coffee maker. Next, I poured in 16 ounces of cool filtered water...

(I'm writing this while the coffee brews. Feeling very sleepy. Super-stoned? Maybe...? Think I'll lie down for, like, no more than a half-hour. Coffee will stay warm on the burner. Check you later...)

Tuesday, October 21- I *must* be sick. I don't feel *horrible*, but I don't feel great, either. Still feeling unnerved; just kind of shaken-up. Let me explain... I woke to the sound of a steady, driving rain beating down upon the roof of The Shack. I remember thinking that our local T.V. weatherman had fucked up again.

I'd thought, 'It's not supposed to rain until Tuesday?!'

I'd had a pounding headache and my stomach was feeling extremely eggy. Anyone reading this who may be wondering what eggy means, it's like being seasick. Nauseous. In need of Pepto-Bismol...like, bad!

On top of that, my back was on fire; burning and itching! I couldn't reach the spot with my hand, although I'd soon realized the irritation was in the general area where that—thing— had raked its savage fuckin' claws across my back! I'd staggered down the hall, to the bathroom...

I'd sort of spazzed out, hit by a sinister idea...

Once in the bathroom, I stood with my back to the sink, looking over my shoulder, into the medicine cabinet mirror. The only thing that came to mind was...

Holy Shit!

There were four, long, red, scratch-marks running from just below my right shoulder-blade; the scratches went diagonally across my back, ending just passed the bumps of my spine. The skin wasn't broken, though. There were only large, red welts. Thank God! Still, they burn like fire, even now, as I write this... I'd shuddered as I recalled my encounter under the levy bridge with that monstrosity. I kept thinking, 'Thank God it didn't break the skin!', even though I don't really believe in God. But it sure couldn't hurt to thank Him, you know, just in case.

After freaking out for about five minutes, my stomach gurgled like a drowning sailor, forcing me to sit down on the toilet. The sailor gurgled, going down for the last count. Then I stunk up the joint...*Royally*! I mean, I hate to be too graphic, but, I took this shit that was *sooooo* gnarly; it was like I'd *crapped* out my whole *innards*! Afterwards, though, that wretched gurgling stomachache had gone away, and I'd felt, like, 30 pounds lighter! W.T.F!

With the exception of my head, which was pulsing in time with my heart, I actually felt *pretty* good.

I was in for a shock...

So I'd walked into the kitchen, feeling like I'd just woken up from maybe a half-hour nap. I'd grabbed some half-and-half from the refrigerator, pouring myself a cup of coffee; I'd stirred in about half a teaspoon of sugar, swirling in a few glugs of half-and-half. I'd raised my mug, saluting the caffeine gods, lips blowing once to cool off the cup of coffee.

I'd taken a quick gulp of my brew—only to spit the funky, stale tasting concoction back up—all over my kitchen counter and floor! It was ice cold!!! And the taste was off. Way off! There was something very wrong with it; both bitter, and *sour*. I'd dumped the rest of the contents of my mug into the kitchen sink, its rancid smell assaulting my nose. I had kind of gagged *and* dry-heaved at the same time, I'd gag-heaved; forcing clear ribbons of snot to come pouring out of my schnozz...

After finally executing a double-nostril-snot-rocket into the kitchen sink, I'd repeatedly rinsed my face with cold tap water. It took every second of a few minutes to recover from that one...

The first thing that I'd done, was to grab the carton of half-and-half, checking its date. October 02, 2014. Well, I guess it *was* quite a few days past its prime. Half-and-half and milk are *definitely* things I prefer fresh; not turning to Cottage Cheese. I'd have to go out to the store. Besides, after looking in the refrigerator, The Shack was definitely *not* holding the snacks. I had all the shit that *gave* you the munchies, just none of the *munchables*...

I'd looked over towards the phone, noticing the answering machine blinking. 13 messages?! I hadn't heard the phone ring once. Not a single time...

I'd pressed play:

"Friday, 3:37 PM," the robotic voice of the machine had announced. It was soon followed by a man's husky voice, "This is a message for Max Whately, concerning the final notification of—"

Beep...

I didn't even want to think about that.

Answering-machine-lady, "Friday, 6:19 PM," Then my mother's voice came over the speaker, "Hey baby, it's Mom. I was thinking maybe we could meet for dinner one of these nights. Give me a call, all right, Max? Bye." I remember thinking she must've wanted to borrow money or something, before skipping to the next message. Beep...

"Saturday, 3:45 PM," followed by... "Hey Max, it's Bill. I was just calling to see if you were gonna go down to the Aquarium, tonight? Sons of Kr'lyrus are playing. It's gonna be pretty heavy, man... Anyway, if you come on down, I was figuring we could throw back a few cold ones. Maybe you could bring that new Ozzy CD down with you, too? (That was his slang for an ounce of weed). Or, maybe, I could just cruise by your place...Whatever's cool for you, bro. Shoot me a call. It's... just...now, uh...hang on, *one* second...It's just now; uh...it's about quarter 'til four. Later dude."

Whoa, what the fuck!? Was it really Saturday afternoon? The rain kept beating down upon my roof...the branches of the Maple trees creaking in the wind. Nature riffing off the storm...

The storm?

After five more messages from that joneser Bill, two telemarketers and three hang-ups (probably "Joneser Bill"); I'd discovered to my shock and horror that it wasn't even Saturday afternoon. Or Sunday for that matter (at that point, a weird panic set in) ...Nope, it wasn't Monday afternoon, either. It was... *Fucking*! Tuesday!! *Afternoon*!!? What in the Hell? Dude! That means, I'd slept for, like, 96 hours or something! Straight on through...

Was that even possible?

I'd quickly decided that, yes, it was possible; seeing as how I was living proof and all.

Damn, as I sit here writing this, pondering my un-natural friggin' nap, it's still raining cats and fucking dogs out there... Just dumping buckets...

At some point, I'm going to have to go out there and brave the elements for some essentials. I'm out of half-and-half. No milk, so I can't make mac & cheese...No chips and salsa...No Fruit Loops. Nothing! Things are looking pretty friggin' bleak. At least I had weed, though.

I just tried to take a bong hit, figuring that it might make me feel better, and my fuckin' lighter just sputtered out and died...Could this day suck any harder? Guess I'm going to have to don the poor-man's poncho, and rough it on the trusty old Schwinn... (For those who aren't fashion forward; using only the finest black Hefty garbage bag, cut hole for head; then, cut holes for arms. Wah-lah! The poor-man's poncho.)

I just got back from the snack-run; this is how it all went down:

So... all suited up for the elements, I'd grabbed the trusty Schwinn from the garden shed, peddling for the corner store. The rain was stinging my face by the time I pulled up to Ye Old Grog Stop. Yeah, that was the *actual* name of the place. The neon Budweiser sign illuminated the dreary, late-afternoon scene. I'd gone through the door, the jingling of bells heralding my arrival. Monty was working behind the counter. He gave me his typical hello:

"Yeah, mon! Jah! Rastafari!" Monty had greeted me with his raspy Jamaican accent. We'd smoked a few spliffs together, on several different occasions.

"Hey, what's up Monty?" I'd replied, keeping it simple... I'm not real big on small talk. I'm weird like that.

"Oh, you know? Lit'le a dis and a lit'le o' dat," He'd said, his island accent thicker than ever. Monty closed his eyes, and began snapping his fingers in an intricate series of clicks and pops. He kind of danced in place while shaking his head, swaying his well-manicured dreadlocks back and forth. Reggae music played on a small transistor radio, tuned to KSEC, the college station. They seemed to dedicate at least 150 hours a week to reggae music.

I'd wandered over to the refrigerated section of the store, grabbing a carton of half-and-half from the back of the cooler, checking the date. As I'd been closing the refrigerator door, a premade breakfast burrito had caught my attention.

"Hey Monty," I'm sure my voice was skeptical, "how long have these breakfast burritos been lurking in here?" I'd called up to the front counter.

"Beats me, mon? I didn't even know we had 'em, Max. But I and I only work in da afternoons, two days a week. Jah bless, soul-jah," Monty had replied, "Jah be keepin' it real for I and I, I'm tellin' you dis mon."

Huh?

I picked the burrito up to, you know, check it out. It was hefty! The burrito was covered in a nondescript, white butcher-paper wrapper. I'd rolled it around in my hand, until I could see the label. Hmmmmm? Intriguing—

A Local brand, more or less...It had been made in Marshville; a burg of a town about 13 miles to the south. There was killer Mexican food down there, though. The sticker had a cool little logo of a skeleton pig. The art on the label had an *El Dia de Los Muertos* vibe. It read:

The Marshville Carneceria
Burrito de Deseyunos:
Huevos, Largo de Cerdo,
Queso, Potatoes & Salsa
Mantener Frigo!
Keep Refrigerated!
24oz.

I brought the breakfast burrito up to my nose and took a deep whiff...I couldn't smell a thing—

It was the last one.

My stomach rumbled once more. I'd grabbed it, rubbed it, tried to comfort it (my stomach, not the burrito), as I continued my trek through the friendly neighborhood mini-market. Suddenly, my gut rumbled with a hideous gurgle. It felt as though a large mass of—something—had plopped from my upper stomach down to my deepest bowels. I'd looked around, embarrassed, hoping there wasn't a cute girl around. Luckily the store was empty, with the exception of Monty and me.

"It's only natural... No worries, bread'ren (brethren)...Da udder (other) night, mon (man)? I and I (he) ate da (the) 'kind (really good) Indian grub; vegan, but da Indian food gives me da farts, mon! Especially da vegan. And I and I only eat vegan. Look out, soul-jah (soldier), I and I still be rippin' da mean ones! Jah, Rastafari," As if on cue, Monty ripped a spicy, Indian-food fart, that brought tears to my eyes...

"Oh, look out for dat one soul-jah... I and I's a Rude Boy!"

"Fuck, man, if you need to wipe your ass, I could always watch the counter for you! Unless, that is, you actually *didn't* just fuckin' shit yourself," I'd grumbled and cussed, continuing to shop.

The smell eventually got so bad, I'd had to stroll outside for a few minutes. With my stomach already sort of nauseous, I'd began dry-heaving at the counter, so I'd quickly sought out fresher air than the wind from Monty's asshole. The rain was still dropping hard from the fat, gray clouds. I'd strolled back in to only a mild hint of Monty's fetid fart cloud. Yuk! I went back outside for a few more minutes, hoping the stench would dissipate completely.

'All right, fuck this noise,' I'd thought.

After a few more minutes, the fresh air finally restored me. My stomachache soon passed. It was time to get some grub and get the F out of there. Recuperated, I'd re-entered Ye Old Grog Stop. These were the things I'd grabbed. You know, the essentials: 2 $1.29 bags of chili-cheese Fritos, a box of blueberry Pop-Tarts, 4 Cup-of-Noodles, a pack of Red-Vines, one six-pack of Coke, a box of Fruit Loops, a half-gallon of milk and a quart of half and half. I threw in a Butterfinger and some peanut-butter cups, along with some beef jerky for protein. A last moment impulse buy. "Yeah, mon! Dat be all den, Max?" Monty had asked.

"No, I need a couple of BIC lighters, also."

Monty brought the little plastic tray containing the lighters out from beneath the counter. With Halloween coming up, I'd grabbed an orange one and a black one. Just to be festive, and all.

"Alright! Yes, I!" Monty punched the prices into the old-fashioned cash register, "Dat'll be… $27.73, soul-jah," Monty said from behind the counter.

I pulled a crumpled up twenty-dollar bill out of my pocket, along with three crisp ones, and a soft, worn-thin five-spot, handing the bills to Monty. He hit a button on the cash register, the cash drawer popping open with a ring. Monty yanked up the little metal bar, placing the crumpled-up twenty-dollar bill on top of a few others, then the five in its respective slot. He shoved the crisp ones into his pocket, before letting the little metal bar snap shut again, handing me back a shiny Quarter, and two dull Pennies. I'd thrust them into my coin pocket.

"Hey, you smoke any o'dat, Velvet Kush? Oh Max, it's so smooooove...reeeeeeeeeeeeeeal smoove, mon!" Monty said, beating on his chest with his fist, adding, "Dat herb be real, Max! Jah... Rastafari!!!" He had begun snapping his fingers, shaking his dreadlocks from side to side, while sort of skanking in place...

"Yeah, it's good! I've got some at home."

"Been pretty dry 'round here lately... Could you maybe sell me a lit'le bit, mon? Like, an eighth?" Monty had asked me.

An eighth? What, were we in junior high? I'd never sold weed to Monty before, but I was always open to new clientele (at least people that I trusted). Besides, as it was, I'd been smoking Monty out once or twice a week for the last few weeks now...

"Yeah, I guess I could break off a little piece for you. 80 bones for a quarter... the Velvet Kush. I don't do eighths though, bro. Sorry. Swing by my place after work. Not tonight, I'm busy," I really wasn't. "Tomorrow night. I'll pack us a few rips, too," I'd told him, gathering up my groceries from the counter.

"Yeah, mon... I and I will see you, tomorrow night, just after 6 o'clock!" Monty enthusiastically replied. "Stay cool, soul-jah. Jah, bless!"

Just then, Robert Goulet, the owner of Ye Old Grog Stop, came busting through the front door. Goulet was a big dude; barrel-chested and burly. His black hair had gone to gray at the sides. He had a large bushy mustache, his eyes piercing blue. I don't think I'd ever seen him *not* wearing a flannel shirt, even on the most blazing hot summer day. Goulet was definitely one tough old geezer; you could just tell by looking at the guy. His name wasn't *actually* Robert Goulet. It was just that he *looked* so much like singer/actor Robert Goulet, the guy could've been his twin brother! The nickname had stuck like glue.

Goulet charged towards me, giving me the stink-eye. He could have been some ex-NFL lineman or a caveman who'd thawed out from the ice-age. Oh shit! Goulet's gruff voice broke the momentary silence of my almost clean get-away. Had he seen Monty pocket the cash?

"What in the fuck is that fuckin' smell? Have you been eating Indian food again, man? How many fuckin' times do I have to fuckin' tell you?! No fuckin' Indian food the night before a fuckin' shift!" Goulet had steered his wrath towards Monty. "This is a God-damned, shared fucking space, that we're trying to co-exist in, mon!"

Now, as much as Monty *wanted* to be a Rastafarian Rude Boy, he wasn't. Monty was a 23-year-old kid, from, as he put it, "Da East Coast, mon!" He wasn't even from Jamaica, New York...

Monty was a *white* kid from Connecticut. So, as Goulet focused his fury upon Monty, Monty had gone from pale-white-kid white, to whiter-than-a-friggin'-ghost white. Goulet sniffed at the air three more times, stating, "No?! There's some other funky-ass stink on top of that...*You* smell like a sewer plant that's been belching and farting all day, but there's also a different...that *weird* smell... like an aquarium full of dead fish," His bulging blue eyes shifted back to me.

"No more Indian food!" Goulet said, giving us both the evil eye, before storming off to his back office. I hadn't realized that I'd been holding my breath the entire time, until I'd let it out.

"Yeah, now dat he said it, I and I *do* smell dat strange fishy smell. How 'bout *you,* Max? You smell some'tin?" Monty asked, scrunching up his nose. "Some'tin really..."

"Just your *ass*hole!" I'd said grabbing my bag of goodies, leaving the wanna-be Rude Boy behind...

I'd peddled off into the rain, steering my trusty Schwinn with one hand, clutching the brown-paper grocery-bag with the other. The bottom of my sack had been seconds away from dropping out, as I hustled in through the back door of The Shack.

That was when I'd first noticed the rank smell; a smell that seemed to linger in each and every corner of my small beach cottage. I lived about two and a half miles from the beach, but The Shack had still been built to resemble a quaint vacation cottage. A beach bungalow. It retained all the style of a 1950's El Cruz beach rental, the predominant features being; small, cramped and drafty. Without the million-dollar view of picturesque Monterey Bay.

Anyways, back to that noxious smell that was, and is, invading my home. Its bouquet is primarily that of sulfuric rotten egg with, perhaps, just a hint of decomposing seaweed. There are notes of left over Chinese-take-out, not so subtly blending with the aroma of spoiled cabbage.

I'd opened the refrigerator door, cautiously exploring the interior; I soon discovered where the malodorous scents of Asia were actually coming from. I quickly collected the offensive culprits; chucking the wretched white cartons, along with half a head of Cabbage-Turned-Jell-O, into the garbage. The garbage bin was pretty ripe, too. Let's not forget, I had just awoken from, like, a 96-hour nap. Like a young Rip Van Winkle. A gagging, dry-heaving, Rip Van Winkle...

I'd grabbed the reeking bag of trash, charging out into the rain, where I'd dumped the stinking sack. Apparently, I had forgotten to take the can to the curb, having completely slept through pick-up day...the stench of *that* nearly bowled me over! After stomping the wretched heap down with my bare foot, I was finally able to mash the reeking trash-bag in. At least, to the point where I could *almost* close the lid of the garbage can down all the way. I'd wiped the slimy gunk out from between my toes, and then dragged my foot across the concrete, trying to finish the job.

When I came back into The Shack, the smell was a *little* bit better; although, there was still sort of a weird stink to it. It was something familiar... I just couldn't quite put my finger on the particular brand of funk. Oh well, Fuck it... Time for a strong cup of coffee!

I ground up some java, dumping it into a brown-paper filter that I'd placed in the coffee machine. After pouring in some water, then flipping the switch, I'd grabbed two of the Pop Tarts, ripping them out of their foil bag with my teeth. I didn't toast them, though; I like Pop Tarts raw, right out of the bag. After a few minutes, the coffee machine beeped. The aroma of the dark, oily liquid, rose to greet my nostrils. The coffee smelled... delicious! I'd grabbed my favorite coffee mug, pouring a steaming 16-ounce cup. I doctored it up just the way that I like it; a little brown sugar, less than a teaspoon, with a few glugs of cream.

I'd grabbed the Pop Tarts that I had wrapped in a paper towel, along with my coffee, and began heading for the living room. My answering machine was blinking again. Three messages since I'd been gone...I'd pressed play:

"Max, what's up? It's Bill. I haven't heard back from you—I was just hoping you were—"

Beep. Next...

"Hey, what's up, Max? Just seeing if you're around. Hope you're okay, bro. I was hoping maybe I could stop by if you're around...You know, grab something? Oh, it's Bill...Right on man I'll see you—"

Joneser! Beep. Next...

"Max...Bill! Hey, maybe you went out of town or something? I really need to see you, shoot me a—"

Fucking joneser!!! Beep. Dude, can't a guy enjoy his breakfast? Speaking of which...

I'd raised the steamy cup of coffee to my lips, inhaling deeply.

Hmmmmm?

The coffee didn't smell as robust as I'd thought it should have. In fact, the coffee smelled a little bit weird, all of a sudden. 'Oh well, fuck it!' (one of my mantras), said the voice in my head. I hadn't had coffee in almost a week! Down the hatch...

The hot, brown liquid, regurgitated back up my throat as quickly as it had gone down! Not because it was too hot, and not because it was too cold. The temperature was just right. The thing was, it tasted like pea-porridge, 3 days old I'd thrown my coffee back up because it was the worst tasting thing I may have ever put in my mouth!

'The half-and-half', I'd thought. That's what it seemed like, vile; disgusting; rancid...dairy! I'd double checked the expiration date on the carton; it still said it was O.K....

That didn't necessarily mean anything. Those dairy farmers, I'm sure, just had to fuck up all the time! Maybe instead of going to bed at 8 PM, and waking up at 4 AM every day, they should try sleeping in every once in a while.

Man, if I could just get some coffee down, I *know* this headache would go away. If I could just get my caffeine fix...

Oh, man…Look who's the fuckin' joneser now!

Shit. I'd figured that maybe my coffee beans had gone bad. I don't know; stale or something. Only worse. It didn't taste good…Not at all. Nope! Not one bit! I imagined that was how raw sewage might taste. Bile had risen to the back of my throat. I'd yakked it back up into the kitchen sink, burning my esophagus. I quickly rinsed both sink and my throat with cool, refreshing water. As I dumped the coffee into the kitchen sink, its putrid smell assaulted my nostrils. My stomach let out a bubbling gurgle. It reminded me of Seymour's voice (the giant, man-eating, plant from 'Little Shop of Horrors'), saying (in a booming voice), "F*eeeeeeee*d M*eeeeeeeee*?!"

I fished out the breakfast burrito I'd recently bought from Ye Old Grog Stop. I tossed it into the microwave, pushing the setting for casserole.

I'd figured, what harm's a little radiation poisoning with breakfast?

Needing a caffeine fix, I had cracked the top of one of the Cokes, guzzling almost half of the soda-pop in one swig. Ahhhhhhhhhhh! Buuuuuuuuuuuuurp!!

Man, oh *man*, was *that* good!!! I'd cracked open the Fritos, munching away on their chili-cheesy goodness. Within the first handful…

Bzzzzzzzzz-Ding! …Ding! …Ding! The hum of the microwave commenced, a high-pitched ringing alerting me that my breakfast burrito was ready for consumption. I'd juggled the piping-hot burrito over to the couch, with chili-cheese stained fingers, sitting down. I'd set the scalding hot burrito on the coffee table, licking my fingers clean before grabbing the remote and turning on the TV. I may be a bachelor, but I still had my pride. I turned on the tube...

Rad! An old episode of Star Trek. The one where Kirk fights the lizard-guy! Oh, it's coming up right now. Whoa, suddenly, the shivers just ran down my spine! I'd begun sweating the second that the screen had flashed on lizard-guy. I'd felt my pulse quicken, followed by a momentary feeling of panic. The fight music had induced a feeling of dread. Paranoia. Da, da, da—Da, da, Da— Da, da, da!

I'd quickly changed the channel, clicking around to see what else was on...I was sweating, my armpits drenched with perspiration.

The daytime talk-show host, nearing 80 years old, but still sporting jet black hair, was just telling white-trash guy, "Bubba... You ARE the father!" Bubba fell hard to his knees crying, pounding his fist into the stage with all his might, a full blown mantrum. The whore-ish looking girl ran offstage; meanwhile, there was an image of the bumpkin baby up on the flat screen, floating above the couch on the set of the talk-show. Bumpkin Baby was a pin-head. Click—

On another station; Two people, well, not really people...they were clowns—actually, I guess clowns technically *are* people—argued their case in front of a female television judge. The judge just happened to be pretty easy on the eyes. Her burly bailiff looked like a jolly Ving Rhames. The entire spectacle had me at hello...

Defendant clown had allegedly broken the nose and three teeth of the plaintiff clown, after the plaintiff clown had made lewd gestures with a balloon, towards defendant clown's girlfriend. Defendant clown's girlfriend was a Russian contortionist, who'd looked like she might also be a sword swallower. Plaintiff clown had (allegedly) asked her to swallow something else. Defendant clown, began demonstrating on an elongated, pink, phallic-shaped balloon! The kind of balloon used to make *balloon animals* for children's *birthday* parties...And this shit was happening on a cable television show! During the daytime! When the balloon finally popped, I'd began laughing so hard, I'd started crying. Then, Defendant clown's girlfriend stood up, tattooed from head-to-toe, bent herself into a pretzel, and swallowed an 18-inch dagger in one fluid, graceful movement!

Oh—My—God!

The shit they put on basic cable these days!? It's fucking insane! I'd grabbed my bong, along with a fat knot of the Ancient Alien Kush. This was the finest marijuana known to man. Breaking off a small piece of the Kush, I stuffed it into the bowl of my water-pipe, sparking it up.

That first hit struck me like a ton of bricks! I'd seen hundreds of black bubbles in my field of vision, feeling like I'd slid 30 seconds forward in time. The strong, skunk-like taste, lingered on my tongue. MMMMM-MMMMMM.

Just for the hell of it, knowing it was going be a lazy rainy day, I'd snapped back a few more, finishing the dense knot of herb. During that time, plaintiff clown's case was dismissed, and he was fined for committing lewd acts against the judge with his long, skinny, balloon... Click—

I'd finally settled on a retro-metal marathon. The trippy old video from the 1970s, for Black Sabbath's, 'Paranoid', was just kicking off...

I'd figured the breakfast burrito had cooled down, at least enough to where I could take a bite. I'd hoisted the thing off the table; cautiously unwrapping the inner layer of plastic wrap from the burrito. That shit could burn the fuck out of you, if you weren't careful. Steam came piping out of the four or five places I'd punctured the breakfast burrito with a fork. It was probably still too hot to eat...I'd let it cool down some more—

After Sabbath, there was a live version of Motorhead's, 'Like a Nightmare', followed by a live version of Metallica's, 'The Thing That Should Not Be'. Off of 'Binge & Purge', I think. Don't quote me on that, though. Up next we had Iron Maiden's, 'Run for the Hills'. I'd gotten this weird feeling that the universe was trying to tell me something—

Around that time, I'd figured the breakfast burrito had probably cooled down enough to eat. Hefting it to my mouth, I took a massive bite. Man, it was pretty fuckin' good! Not as good, as say, a fresh one from Parrot Brothers' Taqueria, but it was still pretty damn good! I'd wolfed that thing down quicker than you can say, "pound and a half breakfast burrito!" Do I have to remind you that I'd gone without a decent meal for a while? I'm still shaking my head over that one... 96 hours? What the fuck?!

I'd finished off the rest of my Coke, finalizing it with another loud belch. After grubbing down, I took a digestive rip off the bong, sitting back deeper into my scruffy plaid couch. The retro-metal marathon had descended into a flaming wreck of lame fuckin' glam-rock—

Click—Click—Click—
Click—Click—Click—
Click—Click—Click—Click.

I'd landed on the Weather Channel. The local forecast was rain, rain... and rain... Followed by even more rain. That was cool. I like the rain...

As I was standing there, out of nowhere, my stomach felt as though it had dropped 3 feet. Then, there was saliva rising up my throat, over my tongue, and flooding into my mouth...

Oh, Fuck! I was about to hurl!!!

I jumped up and ran for the bathroom... I'll save you the gory details, but let's just say that the breakfast burrito didn't live here anymore.

I'd flushed it down the drain.

I felt a little better, though.

After gargling with Listerine, I'd walked back to the couch, wondering what in Hell's name was going on with me. I decided to self-medicate, packing another bowl of the Kush (Hey, what can I say? Marijuana's a wonder drug. It was also one of El Cruz's main exports. The shit just seemed to grow on trees around here).

I'd taken a huge bong rip, getting really high...

Then the phone rang, harshing my mellow. 'Probably that fuckin' joneser Bill', I'd thought.

I have to get caller ID.

After debating; should I, shouldn't I...

I'd snatched up the phone on the third ring.

"Hello?" I'd suspiciously asked.

"Hey, sweetie, how are you doing?" My mother's voice came slurring over the line. Shit-faced drunk; and probably a little high, herself.

"Oh, hey Mom. I'm good...I'm doing well. Just enjoying the rain," I'd drifted off, trying to keep the conversation to a minimum.

"You've loved the rain ever since you were a little boy, you know?" She had cut in. Her voice was a dull monotone.

"I like the sound, it's like... I think of it as nature playing the blues; the howling wind... creaking tree branches. The steady beat of the pounding rain..."

"You want to have dinner tomorrow night?" She'd asked, cutting me off again. I could tell from her voice that she was jonesing for some weed.

"No, I can't make it tomorrow night," I shot back. Let her squirm, "I've got some things to do... the next *couple* of nights," I'd said, leaving it at that.

I haven't seen my mom in almost 2 months. She lives 10 blocks away. The last time we went to dinner together, I'd given her an ounce of weed, just to get her off my back. I haven't heard from her since.

"Well maybe Friday, then? I really want to see you," She had pestered. It had sounded like the monkey on her back was beginning to put a rear-naked-choke hold on her...

"Yeah. That would be fine," I'd lied. "Where do you want to go?"

"How about Stegaro's, out on the wharf. We could have a few drinks...watch the sunset, grab a bite. You know, just have a nice little night," My mother's voice cracked, the monkey now strangling her...

I could just imagine her wild face over the phone, alternating between grimacing and grinning...

She knew I despised seafood. The taste, the smell...the atmosphere! Stinky fucking fish & chip joints, trying to turn their restaurants into a jolly fuckin' pirate ship. Ahoy, mateys! Raise the main sails, and let's call out the galley wenches—Plunder us some wallets—and we'll ravage their land-lubbin' tummies! AARRGGGH!!!

"Yeah. That sounds good," I wasn't about to give her the satisfaction. "That's fine. We can catch the sunset...So...early bird special?" I'd asked.

I could always get a cheeseburger.

"That would be great, honey. Oh... And Max? Could you maybe bring me a little something, if you catch my drift?"

And there it was.

Whatever...

It had been going on since I was 16; almost 17 years now, scoring shit for my mom. Man, it's weird how time flys! Like I said, whatever... it was my mom. I'd bring her a big old bag of growl (high quality bud-shake).

"Yeah see you there...Oh, and mom...I, uh, love you."

On the other line: Click. Followed by that annoying sound that lets you know that the line has gone dead.

Yup, the more things change, the more they stay the same. I'd had a pre-packed bong hit, so I took it. Whoa, black bubbles... Let's do the time warp again. Un-harsh my mellow...

I had turned off the television; I just sat there listening to the rain for a while, before walking over to my drafting table. I sat down in front of a blank piece of paper, determined to do something productive.

I work as a stagehand. It's a seasonal job, and as far as stage craft was concerned, we were heading into the slow time of year; the dead season. It seems like most of the illustration work, my *other* gig, had dried up, too. Everything, that is, except for the weekly arts & entertainment paper, The Best of Times.

There were so many weird sightings in and around El Cruz, that once a month, the weekly rag would either dust off an old case, or spotlight a new one. The column was called "Mysterious Entities". The column was a huge hit in our seaside college town. So, especially for a guy that draws horror stuff, it's been a pretty rad gig.

Over the past three months, there had been three sightings of the same 'mysterious entity', in the lower foothills of the EL Cruz Mountains. During those same three months, a party of five hikers had up and disappeared, somewhere in those mountains. The papers Art-Director had asked me to draw, as he put it:

"A monstrous silhouette, on a full moon night. Make it man-like with burning eyes...two sets of eyes. And shaggy. Make the thing look hairy and unkempt. But, not like Bigfoot... this thing was bigger. Way, way bigger. Oh yeah, and large curving horns, with an extra set of arms and a long thrashing tail"

So, that's what I began working on for the next few hours, getting lost in the creative process of penciling... After that, I began inking the pencil drawing. It hadn't been 15 minutes since I'd began inking, when there came a hard knocking at my front door. It startled me so much, that I'd totally choked the ink line I'd been pulling.

Fuck! I would have to use opaque white ink on that. Then I'd have to let it dry for way longer than I wanted to wait. I'd looked at the clock. 6:30 PM. Could it be Monty? I'd told him not to come by until tomorrow night. Or, maybe that fuckin' joneser, Bill? If it was that goon, Bill...

Whoever it was, I was going to tell 'em to kick rocks. I don't know why, but I decided to look out the peep-hole...I guess you could call it paranoia. I'd puffed enough herb to justify at least a little bit of it...

Holy shit! I couldn't believe my eyes!

Standing on my front porch, looking like some amphibian/man hybrid, was that— Thing!!! That Thing from the levy!!! The gnarly old geezer, ripped like Iggy Pop! That weird creature I'd dubbed "Gog" ...How in the hell did that Thing find me?! I'd stood there frozen, one eye pressed against the door (not *that* one eye. The one on my face). I'd stood as still as a statue.

"Hey, Sonny boy… How's my new favorite little maggot?" Its 80-grit sandpaper voice croaked.

Gog looked mostly manlike tonight; except for the blank eyes, spread far too wide for his gaunt face. It also had four "whiskers" around its mouth. These whiskers weren't hair, but rather, gross fleshy protuberances that reminded me of a catfish. When It spoke, I could see Gog's barracuda teeth; thin, gleaming white scythes!

It may have looked mostly like a man, but It wasn't. This was something that walked in the guise of a man! I'd seen Gog for what he truly was… And he was truly something fuckin' terrible, believe you me!

"What! Cat got your tongue? I ate five or six of those little pussies as a snack on the way over here. Yuuuuummm-mmmmmeeeeee," Gog had rumbled, smacking Its fishy lips; exposing those dagger-like teeth. It continued.

"I can hear you… I can *smell* you, too!" Its batrachian voice nearly crooned, followed by snuffling sounds. Disgusting, snorting-snuffling sounds.

"Just wanted to check up on you… See how things are stewing… Keep you on your tippy toes. So, maggot, how are things stewing?"

I couldn't peel my eye away from the peep-hole. The Thing smiled, ear to fucking ear.

'Shit-eater,' I'd thought, shuddering.

Then, the Thing pressed its eye up to the peep-hole. I'd seen a clear, membranous eyelid slide into place. Its eyes were like empty, white Ping-Pong balls. I'd seen those eyes before, down on the levy. Only this time, there were pale-blue pupils, barely noticeable, focused to sharp reptilian slits.

"I can seeeeeeeeeeeee you," Gog hissed. The man-thing began laughing; a harsh, coughing sound emanating from the creature's chest. It pulled back from the peep-hole, once again standing in full view. Gog flared the gills in Its neck, three on either side. Gog inhaled, the creature's large nostrils flaring open; grotesquely wide… The face of the Thing took on an almost simian aspect. What was it Gog's face remind me of?

A Monkey-Faced Eel! That's what it was. My dad used to catch the creepy looking things up off the north coast. They were extremely ugly, but incredibly tasty! If you've never tried one before, they taste like chicken.

The last time I had encountered him, Gog had looked more like a fearsome Wolf-Eel, yet somehow, this incarnation was *almost* something worse… some parody of the greatest, yet most stupid, of apes. Man.

"See you soon," the Thing said; Its voice cryptic. Gog had turned on a heel, descending the short staircase. In a sing-song voice adding, "Keep on stewing, o'maggot o'mine," before strutting off into the soggy gloom of the wild and woolly evening…

I'd stood there for about three minutes before I'd quickly sought the comfort of my bong.

I'm too shaken up to continue inking the rest of that drawing I was working on. And my headache…

right after Gog showed up, my head began throbbing again. My stomach is also extremely nauseous. Hungry, maybe? Think I'll have a snack, take a few more bong hits, slam another Coke with a few ibuprofens, and then doze off. The rain sounds nice, pounding so hard it almost drowns out my headache, becoming one with it...but what's up with that smell?!!

    Thursday, October 23 (early morning)- I'd risen with a start, making for the peep-hole. Had someone just knocked on my front door? I'd fallen asleep on my scruffy (though comfortable) couch. The rain was still pounding down upon the roof; smacking hard off the pavement. I shot a quick glance at the kitchen clock. 10:45 PM. When had I dozed off? Half an hour ago? An hour?

    Looking out my window, the only thing I could see was the swaying black silhouettes of palm trees, against a charcoal gray sky.

    Was that Thing back? I worked up the nerve to look out the peep-hole. I saw a shape looming on my front porch... Was it Gog? Had he returned to taunt me again? Or something even worse? I'd pulled away from the peephole in a desperate panic. I peered through the hole, taking in the scene one more time. There was definitely something out on my porch. A dark lumbering shadow? A face came into view...

    'Monty? What the hell is *he* doing here?' I'd thought at the time. I'd told him to come by tomorrow night! This was a bit late, even for some wanna-be Rude Boy running around on "Island Time".

But there he was, in his red, gold and green rain get up. He'd been wearing a red rain-jacket with yellow rain-pants, tucked into a pair of green rain-boots. I couldn't help but shake my head in disbelief. I'd opened up the door...

"What the Fuck, Monty? It's almost 11 o'clock at night! And besides... I told you to come by tomorrow night! Beat it dude. Come back tomorrow!" I'd scolded him, scowling.

"Hey, mon!? Relax, Max! Goulet kept me late. I guess it was fate... And besides," Monty's voice stopped bubbling in a faux-dance-hall chant, "what'choo talkin' 'bout *tomorrow* night!? I and I saw you *yesterday*, mon! I and I only stopped by 'cause all your *lights* were on. Includin' da front porch, Max. Sorry, soul-jah, I and I'll come back tomorrow, mon."

I stepped into the soft glow of the porch light, "What do you mean, you saw me yesterday? What day is it?" I'd asked Monty, suddenly confused. I was under the assumption that it was still Tuesday night... My stomach had lurched, heavily, just before my head began swimming. Everything went slow motion for a moment.

"It's Wednesday...Wednesday night. Sorry Max, I-I'll c-c-come back later, y-you don't l-l-look so good," Monty had stuttered. He sounded like he was from Bumfuck, Connecticut—

"No...Sorry man...It's cool. Uh, you want to do a couple of bong-rips?" I'd asked him, inviting Monty in. I'd wondered if he was going to notice the funky smell.

Or maybe Monty was riding dirty, with Indian food streaked undershorts? Yuk!

As he entered my *very* humble abode, The Shack, I couldn't help but notice Monty's nose scrunch up. It was pretty obvious that he'd smelled something foul. It's pretty embarrassing, when a scummy college kid like Monty thinks that your house smells worse than the public landfill.

Kung-Pao hot, Kung-Pao cold, Kung-Pao in the fridge, two weeks old?! Pea-porridge probably would've smelled better. And I hate pea-porridge.

"Sorry about the smell, dude. I forgot about some Chinese take-out, along with a hectic cabbage experiment. The smell's kind of been lingering. I guess I've just kind of gotten used to it," I'd told him apologetically.

"Oh, I was kinda wonderin', mon? Yeah, I and I done dat myself recently, wit' some Indian food. Forgot about da left o'vers. Like some bumbaclot put da voodoo curse on da house for at least t'ree days, Max!" Monty had replied, his Jamaican accent thick. As in, laying it on *way* too thick.

"Well, Let's cover the stink with some stank!" I'd said, packing up my glass water-pipe, and then handing it off to Monty. He'd held the bong aloft in front of him, getting all ceremonial, bowing his chin to his chest; his eyes were closed. Monty took this shit a little too serious...

"Give t'anks and praise for Jah! Rastafari! Hailie Selassie..."

I — momentarily blocked him out.

Monty ignited the sizable bowl, inhaling the giant bong hit deep into his ribcage, holding it for about 20 seconds, before blowing the smoke out. Without coughing! Impressive, but—

Wait for it…and…then…it…hit him. Monty was barking, choking, hacking, then eventually drooling down his chin. "Nice!" He'd declared, before handing the water-pipe back my way. I'd packed one for myself, snapping it through. Hack, cough, hack…black bubbles time…

If this were a movie, this is the part where there'd be some bitchin' classic rock, set to a montage of Monty and me snapping back a *crazy* amount of bong hits. After coughing, laughing, and grubbing down some munchables, complete with a song and dance routine, Monty and I found ourselves back in a smelly smoke-filled room. This wasn't a movie, though. This was my life. We were in the dreary confines of…

My living room.

"So dat's da Ancient Alien Kush? Whoa, mon…*too* gnarly, bread'ren. I and I am seeing black bubbles! You got any o' dat Velvet Kush, Max?" Monty broke the vacuum of space, finally bringing us back down to Earth. Just barely. I wouldn't have sold him any of the Ancient Alien, even if he'd wanted it. That stuff was special… most of it was set aside for another client of mine; And for myself.

"Yeah, definitely…Let me grab it," I'd said, standing, while packing another bowl. I passed the chalice back to Monty. "Be right back…"

I had taken off down the hall to my office; the gurgling of my bong, followed by Monty coughing echoed from the front, as I weighed out a quarter ounce. I threw in a few extra little nuggets. A couple of different strains (hey, what can you say? I treat my people right). I'd scooped it all into a Ziploc baggie.

Returning to my tiny living room, I'd tossed the sandwich baggie of herb to Monty, as he was sitting in a small E-Z chair. He was reclined back, clutching my bong, looking dazed and confused. Monty had seen the black bubbles again. As the sack of herb made contact with his right thigh, he was startled out of his stupor. There were three, crisp $20 bills, fanned out on my secondhand coffee table, along with a bunch of smaller bills. Three of them were crisp one dollar bills, creased in their centers...

Monty looked at me with heavy-lidded eyes, a big, stoned grin taking up his entire lower face.

"Hey, mon...dis is fo' real, brah," Monty was so high he'd switched from Jamaican to Hawaiian. That's what happened when Monty got super-high. "Well, hey, brah...I've got to hit the road, cousin? Yeah? I've got a date wit' dis hot little sista. Hang loose, brah," He'd conveyed the "hang loose, brah" in sign language.

He went on to explain how legendary old-school reggae band, Da Whalin' Spirits, were playing at the Blue. I imagined a bunch of guys dressed like Captain Ahab playing roots music. He'd asked if I wanted to come down. I'd told him no thanks. I walked Monty outside, seeing him off. In his red, gold, and green rain suit, he'd hustled off into the rainy night, as a fresh squall approached from the direction of the sea. Just as I'd gotten back inside, the rain began to pour harder than ever. I'd gagged. The smell of my house was overbearing. My stomach began roiling and rumbling; whether from the smell or from hunger, I still wasn't quite sure.

What had Goulet said?

A smell like an aquarium full of dead fish? Well, that's pretty much what it smells like in The Shack! Despite the smell, I'd managed to munch down a big handful of chili-cheese Fritos, while guzzling down another Coke. After finishing the drawing for the column, I began to work on some drawings in my personal sketchbook. I drew four pages, almost on auto-pilot, covered with macabre figures, by the time I'd finished; monstrosities that I could never show to another living soul. The television had been off for hours, the rain never letting up...just pounding and pounding...

Thursday, October 23 (late night)- The bizarre sensations began early Thursday morning, just as I'd finished my last entry. I was a bit surprised to see that it was 3 o'clock in the morning. I'd been wide-awake; but then again, you would too, if you'd just slept as much as I had, over the last week.

I don't know what had possessed me, but I got the urge to ride out to the ocean. I'd put on a pair of swim trunks, an old beat-up pair of shoes, a hooded sweatshirt, along with the poor man's poncho I had made earlier. I went out to the shed, grabbing the trusty Schwinn, riding off like a phantom into the dark and stormy night. At the true witching hour.

There was no way in hell I was going to take the levy path! Not with Gog out on the loose.

No way, Jose!

I rode down to the river mouth, sticking to the Midtown side of the St. Lorenzo River, peddling through the neighborhoods. It was a gnarly night. The rain kept pouring, flooding the gutters.

After 15 minutes of winding through a labyrinth of streets, I came to Overlook Drive. This majestic old street was lined with Victorians and plantation style estates, standing on the bluff above the St. Lorenzo River. The eucalyptus trees creaked and groaned, their branches swaying in the wind. The old homes were almost all "Painted Ladies", meaning they were decorated in various garish colors, and, pristinely maintained. Overlook Drive was definitely one of the crown jewel neighborhoods of El Cruz.

From here, I could hear the sound of the surf, a low sonic rumble, detonating every five seconds. The rhythmic pulse of the Pacific Ocean! I'd cycled faster...

Another five minutes and I'd come to The Overlook; The Overlook was a large bluff that provided views of the entire Monterey Bay. During the day, the place was a hotspot: surfers checking the swell, beach-betties checking out the dudes, letches checking out the beach-betties, retirees walking their dogs down along the small sliver of Strand Beach. There were also vendor's slinging hot dogs, snow-cones, gyros, soda-pop *and* in some cases cocaine and meth.

You could always tell the vendors that were drug dealers, pushing around their little beat-up, metal carts, covered in ice cream and popsicle decals.

This morning The Overlook was absolutely empty; not even a single parked car in sight. The still, lifeless El Cruz Boardwalk was hunkering below, like the forgotten bones of some colossal beast decaying in the sand, at the ocean's shore. After a few minutes, the rain that had been coming down nearly sideways slacked off to a dreary drizzle. Staring out to sea, I'd been able to just make out the phantom movements of the surging surf. Like ghostly white stallions galloping a frenzied race to the shore, in some phantasmagoric derby...

Whitewater, from the pulsing waves, rushed towards the shore. I'd begun to notice dark shapes gliding through the turbulent surf. I'd sat transfixed as I began to see more and more of these silhouettes; swimming, diving, playfully body-surfing. Like a pod of porpoise, in the shore pound.

Maybe they were seals?

No fuckin' way!

Whatever they were, they were big. Jaws big. They were also numerous... I mean, like, a bunch of them. I lost count pretty quick, being as how it was dark and all. I'm pretty sure I got up to 37 of the things, just as I'd had a brain fart and fizzled out. Then, I'd noticed one of the things body-surf up the river's mouth, riding the foam ball for at least a thousand feet, into brackish water. The tide was high.

I took a narrow path from The Overlook, down to the levy below. I'd peddled my trusty Schwinn as hard as I could, in hopes I'd catch a glimpse of one of those things! Even though I was scared, I couldn't help myself. Something seemed to be drawing me closer.

I'd pulled up to the railing while still sitting on my bike, studying the river some 20 feet below me. After a few seconds, I'd heard water splashing, echoing off the cement retaining wall below me. Now that my eyes had adjusted to the darkness of night, I could make out a large shadow-shape. My mind had tried to wrap itself around what it was seeing...

Even now, as I write this, I have a hard time believing what it looked like. It takes me back to being a kid—

When I was a kid, I'd been to the Steinhardt Aquarium many, many times. In the old days, they used to have a crocodile pit. It was my favorite part of the aquarium. So, I was familiar with what crocodiles looked like; at first, that's what I thought I was looking at. The back of a crocodile. It's not *completely* out of the question for a croc to find its way into the ocean; Not in El Cruz, though. More like Australia...

I'd let out a startled gasp.

It seemed that the creature heard me...

It went from swimming back out to sea, to thrashing around and facing me!

So I'm thinking, 'Holy Shit! I just saw a fuckin' saltwater crocodile off the fuckin' California coast!'... Turned out it was nothing like a crocodile.

I got a good look...

A good *long* look…

I saw the creature's face!

Eventually I saw the whole body.

The hide of the thing had a leathery texture, *like* a crocodile, but the similarities to anything of this earth ended there…What I'd mistaken for an entire exposed back, was only the head of the creature! The top of its fuckin' head!!! I couldn't believe my eyes…

Four glowing green orbs, blinking in unison, stared back at me, reminding me of weird frog's eyes. It had a squashed bat-like nose, triangular with flaring black nostrils. Thick stubby tentacles circled an elongated skull; the thing's gaping jaws were lined with sewing-needle teeth! Its four eyes looked directly into mine, again blinking in unison. Those flaring black nostrils gaped even wider, as it sniffed at the air, tossing its head from side to side. Braying? The mottled gray tentacles that framed the creature's head seemed to move with a life all of their own; one moment sagging like some grotesque fleshy beard; the next, slithering and striking like snapping, demonic serpents. Each tentacle ended with a glowing green eye-orb, casting a soft frenetic light about the creature.

I'd made all these observations in about a 10 Mississippi count—

In the next instant, the creature threw back its head, letting out a wolf-like howl; reverberating off the concrete-wall; off the water below; finally blasting into the early morning, like a thunderous church organ.

Yeah, The Church of Satan, maybe…

Shocked by the electric shivers, all the hairs on my arms stood on end.

Over the steady crash of the surf, I had begun to hear other notes, rising up to join the creature's bass-line howl. Looking out towards the river mouth, my eyes now well-adjusted to the darkness, I could make out several shapes, all different sizes, gliding up the St. Lorenzo River on the foam balls of the dying waves. A shrill air-siren chorus grew louder, as the whitewater washed closer in. Something jumped like a fish, only it was bigger, and sort of shaped like a man.

Sort of...

I saw luminous eyes floating in the dark river; arranged in even pairs of two, four and six. Some of the notes of the strange song were now gurgling and bubbling even closer. There was a weird, high-pitched chittering, accompanied by an even stranger, scarier chattering. I thought of grasshoppers and teeth. Chomping teeth! Grasshoppers with chomping teeth?!

At that point, the rain began to fall harder, again; much harder, than it had rained since I'd left. Fat, wet drops began beating against my face, plunking off my garbage-bag poncho, eventually snapping me out of my stupor—

The thing, with a face like a colossal deep-fried basket of calamari, had begun to pull itself from the river, to the levy's lower edge; first its forelimbs, then another set, followed by yet another set of webbed frog's-feet, and finally its hind legs. I was amazed by the sheer bulk of the thing! Whatever it was, it was a giant! When I last saw the loathsome creature, it was climbing over the rip-rap of the levy, like some alien-elephant-dragon from the bottom of the sea; its tentacles darting into the spaces between the large boulders, plucking out plump rats, then quickly feeding them into its slavering mouth. The smell of deepest ocean, stagnant and foul, was the final impression that the creature left upon me—

Fear, completely took control after that.

I'd peddled off into the early morning darkness, my garbage-bag-poncho crackling in the wind. I was trembling, but not from the cold. I'd quickly put as much distance between me and the sea, as, uhm, humanly possible. There had to be an explanation for what I'd seen down there...for what I'd heard.

Sure, I'd done acid a few times in my 20s, ate mushrooms *more* than a handful of times, and *still* smoked a *lot* of pot. But that *definitely* didn't seem to be a flash-back or anything like that. Come to think of it, I've never really *had* a "flash-back".

I remember hearing something, somewhere, about how mankind knew more about our solar system than we did about the depths of our own oceans. There just has to be all kinds of weird shit from the deeps, still undiscovered by modern science. And just off the shores of El Cruz, is one of the deepest submarine canyons in the world. What, with global warming and all, these things could be affected by climate change. As their own environments are impacted, these creatures would surely have to find new habitats. Maybe this was some totally explainable, natural phenomenon?

Maybe they were migrating...

Yeah that seemed possible.

Who the fuck was I kidding?!

The thing I'd seen was a straight-up monster!

Creature Feature shit! It wasn't the first time I'd encountered something monstrous, down by, or in, the St. Lorenzo River. I'd thought of Gog, as I'd shivered in the wet and windy night. Before I could make it home, the skies opened up once again.

When I'd finally returned to The Shack, the sun was about an hour or so from coming up. I'd figured I'd just write in my journal, but passed out instead. Just woke up, it's still a few hours from midnight. I don't know why, but I'm feeling very strange, a fluttering in my stomach. Nauseous...Stomachache has come back, along with the throbbing headache.... I Need to use the toilet...

I've just returned from the bathroom, where I'd vomited up, and shit out, God only knows what!? Caught my reflection in the mirror, and I *definitely* look like there's something *wrong* with me! Something bad.

Done writing for the night. A few bong hits, a little tube, and then I'm going to check in for some shut eye; get some rest...

P.S. – I had bought a new half-and-half from the grocery store and made a strong cup of coffee earlier, only to instantly gag it back up. If I could just get a cup of fuckin' coffee down, I know this God–damned fuckin' headache would go away. Maybe I've become lactose intolerant, or something? Need to make a doctor's appointment, first thing in the morning!

Friday, October 24- I'd started awake in a panic, a flood of sunshine streaming in through my window. The sunlight seemed to quickly wash away any deep feelings of dread that I'd been having.

Until...

As I'd rolled out of bed, there was a strange rustling sound. I had touched my hands to my rib cage, giving an involuntary cry, as my hands were met with a strange plasticized skin; skin that felt as though it were crinkling and sloughing away from my body!

Holy-Fucking-Shit-What-The-Fuck?!!!

You can only imagine my reaction (total fucking idiot!), when I'd realized; I wasn't a man morphing into an insect, or anything exotic or bizarre like that. I was just some jerk who'd fallen asleep wrapped in a Hefty garbage bag. After quickly shedding the Poor Man's Poncho by shredding the thing from away my body, I'd grabbed my bong, using it as a Band-Aid for my bruised ego. One snap, two snaps, three snaps, four... I think I'll puff a couple more!

I'd picked up my favorite coffee cup from the counter of the bar, walking over to the coffee maker. Alright, time to try this again. One more time. At this point, my headache was only the slightest little thrum, throbbing in time with my pulse. In time with my heart. Anyways, what was I saying about coffee?

I poured some whole coffee beans into the grinder, whirling them away to a fine brown powder. With the grinder at full wail, I finished my rocket launch countdown to 19. I brought the coffee-grinder to a grinding halt. First, you use 5 heaping tablespoons coffee, plus one for the pot; like tipping a little malt liquor out for your homie. Then add 16 ounces of cool filtered water. I'd pushed the single cup button, then flipped the brew switch—

A few minutes later, and, abracadabra. I *should* have a mean cup of strong Joe. My headache had returned, pulsating through my temples; inside my forehead. Out of nowhere, my stomach made a wet gurgling rumble; followed by that now all too common, instant wave of nausea.

Yum, coffee! I guess I'm just a glutton for punishment. 'I should try to eat something,' I'd thought. Suddenly! An uncontrollable fart, fetid and foul, came bubbling out of my ass. Smelling of boiled eggs and broccoli?! Something moist spattered my inner thighs...Oh, Shit!!! Not really, but I'd freckled my boxer shorts...That's right! I'd sharted!

I'd scrambled down the hallway to the bathroom, scuttling like an enormous crab. Through a series of grunts and groans, I'd really tried to let those little toilet-fish swim free. But alas...there I'd sat brokenhearted, tried to shit but only farted...And say, have you heard the one about the guy from Nantucket? I cleaned the spatter. The wave of nausea washed over me as quickly as it had come (gnarly tube-ride, bro!). I'd risen from my porcelain throne, standing before the sink. I had thoroughly washed my hands with soap, and piping hot water.

The whole thing was an event that called for full-on minutes of splashing ice cold water on my face.

I'd tossed the boxers in the bathroom garbage can. Eventually, I'd have to take that fuckin' shit out.

The stench of ass, blended with fisherman's wharf, hung over my bathroom. In fact, the smell of the entire bungalow had been pretty ripe as of late.

Extra-ripe!

I'd have to air out The Shack. Definitely time to flush the cabin. Out with the bad air, in with good... From the kitchen I'd heard the coffee maker beep. Then I'd looked into the mirror!

Jesus H. Christ on a popsicle stick! I looked fucking terrible! And by terrible I mean *horrible*...The skin over my *entire* body was dry; peeling. Like after a sunburn. I hadn't been in the sun in a while. What the fuck? Along with the sudden skin condition, my hue had taken on a weird, white-blue color. Like the color on the belly of a rock cod. A Capazone...The color of Gog?! Shivers ran down my spine! It was about this time, that the sore throat began to set in.

I began taking deep breaths...Out with the bad air...In with the good ...Out with the bad air...In with the—Disgusted, I'd hopped into the shower, quickly vomiting while hoping to wash Gog's taint from my flesh. Not taint as in, taint my balls and taint my ass, but, you know... like, Gog's filthy touch...

Oh God! There had been those welts across my back! I'd scrubbed certain body parts until I had strawberries. I'd vomited a second time; then a third! The water was too warm, so I'd turned it down until it was ice cold. I couldn't believe how good the frigid water made me feel. Time stood still. Minutes seemed like hours. Rejuvenated from the healing power of the shower, I finally stepped out of the tub. I caught a reflection of my body in the mirror. Damn, I'd lost a lot of weight over the last week... An *unbelievable* friggin' amount. Something was wrong... Something was *definitely* wrong. And was the smell from The Shack actually emanating from me? I'm starting to seriously wonder.

Just as I'd begun brushing my teeth, there'd been a series of sharp pains in my neck. First one, followed by another, and then another, again. There were six in all. Three upon each side. Strange wattles of skin; weird iguana-like skin? The things were definitely sore, looking as if they could almost burst open at any moment. Like...

Gills?

As I'd finished brushing my teeth, at the back of my neck, where it meets the shoulders, there was a single popping sound!? I cried out in pain! The pain quickly subsided. I'd glanced in the mirror one more time. It seemed as though my neck had stretched out a bit! Like, it had gotten a little longer...But my stomachache seemed to have gone away, at least.

Now, if I could just lose the fucking headache.

I'd walked down the hall to my bedroom, flinging on some clothes, then messing up my hair. Even though I'd just washed it, my hair felt greasy... And thin!? As I'd pulled my hands away, clumps of hair had come with it. I threw my hair to the ground in dismay. The shock was apparent on my ghost-white, blue-tinged face, as I'd gazed into my bedroom's mirror. My once full head of hair, now has visible thin patches. Through the thin patches; weird little wart-like bumps?! Things that look like fish-scales, too! What the FUCK!!? God! And the smell? Is that me? I'm pretty sure it is...It fucking can't be me...Still in shock, I'd walked into the kitchen, and poured myself a cup of coffee. My coffee machine has been kind of frazzled lately, occasionally turning itself off after the brewing process. It seemed like that's what had happened again today. I drank the coffee in one long gulp...And it was cold. Ice cold! What in the hell?!Looking around the room, my eyes focused on the stove's digital clock. 4:30 PM!? What time had I woken up? How long had I been on the toilet? How long had I been in the shower? How long had I been walking around my bungalow in a daze?! Where is that rank smell coming from? Then I remembered—I'm supposed to meet my mom at Stegaro's tonight. In half an hour! Wow, all of a sudden I just got real hungry! I've got to get ready to go. Jesus, I look like hell, though?! And The Shack is stinking to high heaven. Even with windows wide open. Maybe something I've missed in the 'fridge? Went to investigate, only to turn up empty handed. What's that fucking stench? Is it me? No, it couldn't be me...It's the smell of an animal, not a human—

Fuck it, I'll have to deal with it when I get home. I'll put on my rain hat to cover my face, and a raincoat to hide my arms. God, my throat fuckin' hurts...I'll deal with it latter—Got to run—

This was the last entry from Max Whately's Journal...It's interesting to compare with this article in the 'El Cruz Inquisitor', from the following morning's newspaper:

El Cruz has long been a town with many a weird happening. And last night's event will probably go down as just another, on a long list of strange occurrences, in El Cruz. Like most of these bizarre situations, last night's attack at Stegaro's, located at the very end of the EL Cruz Municipal Wharf, would end in the loss of life. This was the eyewitness account of El Cruz senior citizen, Howie Phillips, who watched the entire thing unfold from his table, no more than 5 feet away:

"The woman seemed ordinary enough. She was probably 60 years old. Dressed casual. I don't mean to sound harsh, but she looked like the kind of lady that had lived a hard life. There are a lot of those types of ladies around here. But the guy? Or whatever that was that came in? That guy gave me the willies! Dressed like a fisherman drowned in a storm! I'm talking some real heebie-jeebies. And the smell? It was worse than an entire drum circle of those reefer smoking dirt-bags, mixed with cat food. The canned, wet, smelly kind. Or tuna fish! I'm originally from the East Coast. We used to eat a lot of tuna fish, so I know the smell of tuna fish!" Mr. Phillips had stated, quickly adding, "I don't touch the stuff anymore, though. I despise seafood. I only come out here for the view, along with a few drinks at happy hour. Keepin' an eye out for frog and fish men."

Stegaro's. This legendary restaurant, the very last restaurant, at the end of EL Cruz's Municipal Wharf, offers beautiful panoramic views of the

Monterey Bay Sanctuary. It has long been a favorite haunt, for both tourists and locals alike. *The* place if you want to check out the wild surfers, riding the waves off Ghost Train Point, while enjoying an award-winning cup of "Stegaro's world-famous clam chowder". For a more sophisticated crowd: Watch the sailboats of the Wednesday night regatta, over a delicious, lightly-breaded, grilled lemon sole (served with capers, red onions and parsley-butter. Includes dinner salad with rice-pilaf), paired with a glass of Chardonnay (This reporter's favorite! Yum…) That's what goes on at Stegaro's most every night. A wonderful dinner experience. But last night? Last night, with the rain pouring down, and the fury of the surf surging in from the Pacific Ocean, these were the words of waitress, Wanda Holdscock:

"I was just approaching the table. It was a window booth. On a clear night, it would've been a nice view. All you could see tonight was rain coming down sideways. I had just picked up their food, and, like I said, I was approaching their table, when the guy stood up and started taking his clothes off! Like, totally off! When he came in and sat down, he'd been wearing a big, floppy, yellow rain hat. It had been hiding his face the entire time he'd been sitting there. Not very long, really… About 20 minutes, maybe? The guy's body was weird looking, like…really weird? Once he had stripped down to his boxer-shorts, he'd reached for the hat. That's when I'd noticed his hands. They were gross! Like a frog, with claws, sort of? I'd quickly glanced at his feet. They were the same. I just screamed. All of the customers stopped eating. It was, just, totally quiet. You could hear the waves rolling under the wharf, the rain gushing down outside…then, the guy lifted up his rain hat?! That guy had to be wearing a Halloween mask, or something!? He just had to be!??" Miss Holdscock had made this statement before becoming too hysterical to continue. It was floor manager, Jack Collins, who'd seen the final events in its entirety, as he had come to Miss Holdscock's rescue. These were his observations:

"If that thing was a mask? Then that mask came out of Hollywood! Period. And they would've needed a crew of people to help him put that thing together! I saw the things eyes blink. Its nostrils flare…I know they've got air bladders to do all of that stuff, but… I saw its face as its lower jaw unclamped! And those teeth! Such sharp, thin teeth…Those teeth…I saw it, as it sank those teeth into the lady's face! And then— and…then, it— and then it tore her face away!!! Everything! Flesh…bone…her teeth, her nose, her eyes…All of it! Just a horrible crunching sound… At that point, I could tell Wanda was out on her feet. Like a million miles away. As I'd moved in, grabbing her arm, the thing howled at me. Oh, and the smell! The smell was… like…It was like rotten kelp, lying on top of sewage. I pulled Wanda back to the bar. A weird series of cracks and pops sounded off through the guy's whole body. And then he changed! Like, transformed!? Like I said, I know they have air bladders and special effect tricks, but not for that. Stuff like that's done with CGI nowadays. The guy went from being wide, like a man… To narrow, like a fish! His body mass was pretty much the same, just weird looking! Really, really, (expletive) weird looking. Probably about 220 pounds. With the elongated neck, the thing was close to 7 feet tall! The guy had only been about 5'7" when he walked in…the thing...just wolfed down the face of that poor lady, so (expletive) fast. She got up and began wobbling around the dining room. It was (expletive) chaos, customers were screaming. Running for the exit—it was a total (expletive) nightmare—then, there was another round of cracks and pops, then, the things neck telescoped out. The things terrible jaws (expletive) clamping down on top of that poor woman's head! In an instant, the thing crashed through the window, diving out into the ocean, dragging off that poor (expletive) lady along with it! It was like watching a large predator taking down much smaller prey."

There was no identification found in the discarded clothing. As of early this morning, no bodies have been found. The fish-man is still at large. The glass has been swept up. The broken windows will be fixed. The blood scrubbed clean. El Cruz Surfers will continue to amaze tourists, performing their dazzling aerial acrobatics off the point of 'Ghost Train Point'. The bright, cheery sailboats will continue racing the Wednesday night regatta. And tourists will surely keep flocking to Stegaro's, for a cup of their world-famous chowder; Or, perhaps, the beloved Treasure Chest Seafood Platter...But, to the sound of driving rain, with the booming surf thundering in from across the Pacific Ocean, all the lights turned off along the wharf's popular storefronts; Tonight this reporter wonders:

Will last night's event, that strange occurrence at the legendary Stegaro's, at the end of the EL Cruz Municipal Wharf, overlooking the beautiful Monterey Bay Sanctuary...Will that mysterious attack, and disappearance, ever be fully—completely—explained?

Best of Times

El Cruz Seaside Diner

Chef's Special*:

Still Hungry for a Bit More?

Well, how 'bout some ???

CORNED BEEF HASH

Snab it or Grab it

Collection Exclusive!!!

Secret Recipe!!!
Secret Recipe!!!
Secret Recipe!!!

* May contain dispicable content?!!

Corned-Beef Hash

I f it weren't for bad luck, Seamus O'Toole wouldn't have had any luck at all. Oh, I know what you're thinking; luck of the Irish and all that dribble, but –

Nope! There would be no such thing, for poor Seamus. His various misfortunes were many, accumulating a list far too miserable, and lengthy, to account for here; his missteps, his indiscretions, were all very well documented by the Marshville Sherriff's department. As is often the case with many juvenile delinquents, Seamus grew to become a delinquent adult, as well. By the time he was 21, Seamus O'Toole, through addiction and abuse, had become a wretched creature to behold, merely the husk of a being.

There had been his inevitable descent into various narcotic cocktails, always washed down with cheap booze. This lead to Seamus eventually living rough, on the mean streets of Marshville. Once he was homeless, it seemed as though his encounters with the Sheriffs were both many, and varied; Eventually,

Seamus' downward spiral landed him in prison. The Big House. Who would have thought that beating one of his drug dealer's thugs, nearly to death, and the subsequent jail sentence, would be the turning point in Seamus' life? But it had been. They'd got him on a bunch of other counts, too. Possession of narcotics, paraphernalia, intent to sell and distribute. They sentenced Seamus to 12 years. Pelican Bay.

Seamus had been forced to get clean and sober while living behind bars. It had been the first time in quite a few years that Seamus had eaten 3 square meals a day. No matter how terrible the other inmates claimed that the food was, it still beat his dad's specialty; Freezer-burned Hungry Man's T.V. dinner. That was if Seamus' dad decided to cook at all when he was a kid, which was hardly ever. So Seamus didn't really mind the food.

While serving his time, Seamus received dental work that law-abiding, tax-paying members of society paid for; along with free education, also payed for by those same law-abiding, tax-paying citizens. He'd become an electrician. So that had all worked out pretty well for young Seamus. Free Education!

One might even say that his luck was changing.

Seamus had even made some friends, while serving his time in the Super-Max facility. A whole gang of them. All he had to do to hang out with these guys, was get a tattoo, to show his loyalty. So he did. Seamus had asked his tattoo guy to give him a good luck symbol, like, maybe a four-leaf clover, or something like that. Tattoo Guy assured Seamus he had just the symbol in mind. Seamus was horrified, when he finally looked at his brand new tattoo in the mirror; a solid black swastika covered his entire shoulder.

"What the fuck?! I said a good luck symbol!" Seamus had hollered at Tattoo Guy.

"That *IS* a good luck symbol. For starters, It's gonna keep you from gettin' boned in the shower. How's that for luck?" Tattoo Guy said, a shitty grin covering his ugly mug. "Besides, if it really bothers you, think of it as Hindu. It is. And that's God's honest truth," The grin had left Tattoo Guy's face, replaced by a look that could almost pass as solemn...After getting the tattoo, all the guys were really nice to Seamus, though. It wasn't until his first parole hearing, that the tattoo *really* began to haunt him. On that day, he was whisked away into a room where his tattoo was photographed. When he returned in front of the board, Seamus was told he was being denied parole, due to his affiliation with an Aryan prison gang. As far as his luck, that had taken two steps forward, one step back concerning the tattoo (it *had* kept him from getting butt-fucked in the shower, so there *was* that). But it had been that God-damned tattoo, time in and time out, that denied Seamus parole; over, and over, and over, and over yet again! But Seamus continued to toe the line...

And then, after his seventh review, Seamus finally got word that he was being let out on parole, for exemplary behavior. 2 more weeks behind bars, then he was a free man.

***

Tonight would be the last night he slept behind penitentiary walls. He'd dozed off quickly, falling into a dream about his 9th birthday. It had been a great birthday, the last wholesome memory of his tainted adolescence. His dream was just like it had been in real life; his dad had tossed him a box of Lucky Charms and told him, "Happy Birthday, kid. Knock yourself out,", Before storming out of the house. Seamus' 9th birthday had been on a Saturday, and back in those days they showed cartoons 'til noon. So Seamus had sat around eating bowl after bowl of Lucky Charms. After the 4-hour block of cartoons, there was always 2 old monster movies on, back-to-back. Seamus munched down handful after handful of delicious sugary cereal like it was popcorn while watching those. Another 4 hours went by in an endless stream (with exception to commercial breaks) of women's blood-curdling screams, dramatic organ music crescendos, and all sorts of growling and snarling, in high-contrast black & white. After the Monster Madness & Mayhem Marathon, Seamus watched his dad's cable channel, the one he wasn't supposed to watch; he thought it was called Skin-A-Max, or something like that. It was while committing this forbidden taboo act, that Seamus had finished off his birthday present. That box of cereal that had been so delicious; Almost magically so.

The dream up to this point was exactly how events had actually been on Seamus' 9th birthday. But this is a reoccurring dream, and Seamus knew where this was all going. In his dream, he scrambles for the remote, frantic to change the channel as he hears a rumbling out in the driveway. Everything seems like it moves in slow motion, his fingers fumbling for the right button, heavy footsteps coming up the shoddy wooden stairs. Seamus finds the button with his thumb, clicking it, changing the channel to a Brady Bunch re-run. Just in the nick of time. Seamus listens, then hears the front door swing open, hard, smashing against the interior wall. He sees his father's shadow swaying across the wall of the hallway, before he actually sees his father. The dream is always like this...

And no matter how many times Seamus has this same dream, He's always surprised when it's not his father that comes staggering out of the hallway, but Lucky the leprechaun. A giant, rabid, angry version of Sir Charms. The giant cartoon rushes up to the empty box of cereal. Lucky picks it up, savagely shaking it up and down, the last few morsels of cereal flinging about the room. There isn't a single—not one—crunchy, colored, marshmallow left. "You ate all of me Lucky Charms?!" Lucky screamed, his whisky breath a gust upon Seamus' face. Lucky went from an already Bashki-like version of himself, to a full blown Rat-Fink; sharpened teeth, lolling tongue, dripping saliva and bulging eyes not excluded...Lucky-Fink was smoking a Lucky Strike cigarette.

"You little son of a bitch! I wish I could shut you up, like I shut your mother up," Lucky-Fink spoke in Seamus' father's voice, "shut her up for good!" he growled, grabbing 9-year-old Seamus by the wrist.

When the Rat-Fink leprechaun made contact, Seamus remembers a skull, its teeth pulled from their sockets, that had been found in a construction-site dumpster down the street from his house, when he was 4. Because his dream is reoccurring, he always remembers his wrist snapping under the pressure of the leprechaun's grip a second or two before it actually happens; same thing with the cigarette burns from the Lucky Strike. Seamus always wakes up, just before the glowing orange cherry touched his cheek.

***

Seamus wakes up to a dirty grey light, his finger drifting up to the circular pock mark on his cheek; his only proof that that night had actually happened. He only remembered his dream for the first 10 seconds or so upon waking. That was how it always was. He rubbed his aching wrist, the one he'd mysteriously awoken to find with a cast on, the day after his 9th birthday. He'd blacked out and had no memory of how he'd fallen victim to a broken arm and a cigarette burn on his face, that night. He only had any kind of idea in those first 10 seconds...

Seamus shook the fog of his nightmare off, forgetting it altogether before long...

After a shit, shower and a shave, Seamus had been given his old street clothes back. They'd been laundered, and they still fit. After that, he found himself at the collections desk, where he received an old Casio watch along with a nylon wallet. The watch's battery had died and his old wallet had $2 in it, crumpled and torn. Upon leaving, Seamus was given an envelope with $525. That was $75 a year, for every stinkin' year he'd spent in the joint, working in the laundry-mat. 'It's better than a thumb in the eye, though,' Seamus told himself.

By mid-morning, Seamus was doing circles out on the concrete in front of the prison, in a sort of daze. There was no one there to greet him. Dad had died during his first year inside, and wouldn't have come, anyway. It took him a few minutes to compose himself and gather his thoughts. Seamus pinched his forearm, to reassure himself this wasn't a dream. He was free.

Seamus was 30 years old. Still a young man, but a man none the less. Seamus glanced back at the butt-ugly building, surrounded by multiple perimeters of razor-wire, topping the fence. He'd matured a lot behind all that fucking barbed-wire.

Facts were facts, though. Seamus had no family, no friends, no home to return to, and no prospects. Seamus didn't have any—

Seamus had almost thought 'hope', as he automatically shut down his inner voice; like his prison appointed therapist had taught him to do. To give something thought, was to give it power. Seamus O'Toole was a new man...a new man whose luck was changing. It was his own personal mantra...

With $525 in an envelope stuck in his front pocket, Seamus struck off on foot to find the Greyhound station. About 15 minutes into his walk, his stomach began to rumble. It wasn't that he was hungry; he needed to use the toilet. Another few minutes brought Seamus stumbling up to a Chinese restaurant that, as luck would have it, happened to be open for breakfast.

Upon entering the garishly-red painted building accented with peeling gold-trim, Seamus was hit with a waft of deep-fried stench. An elderly Chinese lady, who could have been anywhere between 95 and 150 years old, frowned at Seamus, asking him in a harsh, raspy voice, "What you want?"

"Bathroom?", Seamus asked.

The frowning old hag pointed to a sign that read: RESTROOMS FOR CUSTOMERS ONLY! Seamus looked past the wrinkled little apple-witch, to the diner style menu board. It was the kind with the raised plastic letters, see-through red, that would have been found in a diner. He found it rather odd that the words Breakfast, Lunch, and Dinner were snapped on to the board in English; everything else was Chinese characters. The prices were numbers, so... Seamus quickly scanned the menu board, zoning in on the cheapest thing on their breakfast menu. He ordered that. The little Chinese lady's eyes grew wide. "You sure want that?!" She said, shaking her head; she began to chuckle. Seamus' stomach grumbled. The smell of the place was making him feel sick.

"Yeah, to go please, ma'am," Seamus said, shuffling off towards were he thought the bathroom should be. He was stopped in his tracks.

"Wait!" the old woman screeched, "You pay now!" She was a pushy little thing, she was. Seamus hobbled back over to the ancient crone, doubling over at the waist. "Seven dollar ninety-seven cent!", her tone sharp and angry. Seamus fished out his envelope and pulled out a crisp $10 bill, handing it over to the Dragon Lady.

"Change?" She snorted. It was a defiant question, asked with a venomous stare.

"No, keep the change. Restroom?"

The mean old lady nodded her head, in the opposite direction, of where Seamus had originally thought the bathroom to be... He quickly made a run for the bog, each footfall a sharp dagger to his bowels.

10 minutes later Seamus returned to the counter, with a little more pep in his step. He was even considering *eating* the food he'd just ordered. As he came within arm's reach of the cash register, he was startled by a high pitched singing. The old lady must have been back in the kitchen. The sharp, warbling song, small and sweet, drew Seamus' attention to a small cage on the register counter. Inside was a furry little creature, with huge expressive eyes, it's ears pointy; the creature was the source of the whistle-like

tune. Suddenly, the old lady came bursting out of the kitchen, then limping up to the register counter; the strange, fascinating creature continued to sing.

"You touch my register?!" she yelled, eyeballing Seamus. The little singing creature changed keys...

"No," Seamus shook his head, almost adding 'I just got out of prison and don't want to go back', then deciding just to leave it at that. The creature changed keys again, squealing and chirping its song. "What is that thing?", Seamus asked in a hushed tone.

"Furby! Now scram!" She thrust the plastic bag, containing the stinky food, at Seamus, waving her arms towards the door as soon as he'd grabbed it.

Another 5-minute walk found Seamus at a small corner park, the once bright-green grass having long turned to hay. There was a sand box with a toy crane shovel, and a wobbly sea-horse on a giant, not-so-tightly coiled spring, leaning heavily to one side. The only other decorations; a square waste bin, covered in tiny pebbles, many of which were missing; and a concrete bench, nestled between an unruly bunch of dense, wild scrub, that backed up to a stagnant drainage ditch, trying very hard to pass itself off as landscaping.

Seamus decided to take a seat on the bench, checking out his Chinese take-out breakfast. He was hoping that the smell was deceiving, as can sometimes be the case with food. He removed the balsa-wood chopsticks, container and fortune cookie, the smell intensifying (and not in a good way) as Seamus opened the bag. As he unfolded the white take-out carton-lid back, a nauseating waft of warm air came steaming up into his face. He immediately broke out in a cold sweat... Seamus gagged. He couldn't tell which was worse; the smell of the take-out, or, of the drainage ditch. He decided it had to be the food. Yuck!

Out of horrified curiosity, Seamus probed the cardboard carton, red Chinese temple printed on the side, with his balsa wood chopsticks. He eyed black pickled eggs with putrid green yolks, sliced over what could have been either mushroom, or pancake. Some sort of things, that looked like scorpions, shiny and black, had been smothered in a bright red glaze and rested atop the mushroom/pancake thing. This all sat upon a mound of rice; everything was covered in an oily-brown gravy, that smelled like canned tuna fish. He grabbed the fortune cookie, and stuck it in his coat pocket.

Rising from the bench Seamus walked over to the trash can. As he was preparing to toss the food in the can, his attention was drawn back towards the bench. The overgrown bushes were a-sway with activity. Just to the left of the concrete bench, the bushes parted; There, a large figure pushed themselves through the entanglement of brush.

It was a man, though whether because of disease or deformity, Seamus had never seen anyone quite like this man before. As the man waddled up to Seamus, he was able to make better observations of the man's strange features. His head was hairless; no eyebrows or eyelashes either. The man's eyes seemed to be spread too far apart; his nose squashed nearly flat; his mouth, far wider than it should be. He wore a beige trench coat and Seamus began to wonder if the dude was going to flash him. At least he didn't have to look at the weirdo's obviously twisted and lumpy, misshaped body. The man curiously sniffed at the air as he drew nearer. The only other parts of the strange man that were visible, were the creep's hands; calloused horny things that reminded Seamus of The Creature from the Black Lagoon, without the talon-like nails. The weirdo's nails *were* jagged, feral and overgrown, but otherwise human looking. *Like* The Creature from the Black Lagoon, the strange man had what could only be called webbing, spread between fingers and thumb. He wore dirty white Converse Chuck Taylor's on his massive feet. They had to be at least size 16, and wide. The weird transient began humming to himself. He was clammy, and his aroma definitely matched his pallor; Stagnant, almost as though he'd come from the dirty drainage ditch.

Seamus' prison-yard senses quickly kicked in; he'd had seven long years to hone them. "Hey, what's up man?" He asked the weirdo, his voice dropping an octave lower than normal. That was a trick his dad used to use on him, back in the day.

"Smells like my mom's cookin'. *De-li-cious*! Say... it looks like you're going to toss that," the weirdo answered. Seamus didn't know what to make of the dude's voice. It was warbled; modulated and wet sounding. Phlegmy. It also seemed like two voices speaking at once; One voice, Seamus could feel in his chest; the other so shrill as to be ear-piercing. "If you are, can I have it?" the strange man asked, in that vertigo-inducing, double-octave voice.

Seamus handed the carton over to the poor misfortunate creature. The weirdo went scuttling back towards the bench, entering the bushes at the spot from which he'd emerged. Seamus took the Fortune cookie from his coat's pocket, peeled off the cellophane wrapper, throwing it in the old pebbled garbage can. He reminded himself that the old Seamus would've thrown that wrapper on the ground. He cracked open the stale cookie, pulling the strip of paper from the baked fold of dough. Glancing at the fortune, it read: You would do well to follow the rainbow! (on the reverse side, Lottery numbers: 7, 13, 21, 33 & 77). Seamus folded the tiny strip of paper in half, sticking it into the coin pocket of his jeans. As Seamus departed, he thought he'd heard something large splash down in the stagnant drainage ditch. He hurried along his way down the street, away from the sad little park.

Seamus happened to look up at the sky, spotting a weak, washed-out rainbow. He decided to follow it, remembering the story of leprechauns, and pots-o'-gold from his childhood. Another couple of minutes walking brought him into the downtown area, the hazy little rainbow terminating just over the Greyhound terminal.

As Seamus made his final approach to the bus station, a gust of wind came blowing in from the opposite direction, kicking up a dust-devil to block Seamus' path. Small dried leaves, along with carelessly discarded litter, spun within the vortex of the miniature tornado. And upon this weird wind, floating round and round in circles, was an unused bus ticket. As quickly as it had begun, the dust-devil petered out, depositing the bus ticket at Seamus' feet. He bent down, picking it up. Seamus scanned the immediate area, looking for someone franticly searching, patting their pockets or rifling through their bag; anyone in some sort of mild distress. The sidewalk was empty on this side of the street. The few pedestrians that were out, walked with their attention focused on their mobile phones, in quick, purposeful strides. Thinking maybe someone may have reported a lost ticket, Seamus decided to poke his head into the bus terminal. The place was absolutely desolate, with exception to a cadaverous senior citizen who was sitting behind a plastic window; obviously the ticket salesman. The wrinkled old mummy of a man, never looked up from the battered and worn paperback that he was reading; Richard Bachman's, 'The Regulators'.

Seamus exited the station, taking his first real look at that bus ticket he'd found. It was a coach ticket, destined for El Cruz, California, with a departure time of 3:30 pm. In the ticket's corner, there was a square hologram that blazed the colors of the rainbow when he tilted it this way and that. El Cruz was only about 15 miles (13 to be exact) north of Seamus' home town of Marshville. That settled it. Seamus would be taking the bus to El Cruz this afternoon. He glanced around, finding the bus terminal's clock; 10:30 AM. He had some time to kill...

Seamus walked the length of the dusty little downtown area. A few minutes later, he came upon a café that shared a space with a tiny, independent movie theatre. Intrigued by a split-image poster, Seamus decided to buy a ticket for an 11:00 show. Back before he'd began living rough, he'd had a friend named Obie; Seamus and Obie would smoke pot together, listening to old scratchy vinyl records. Obie's folks had tons of records. It was at Obie's house that he'd first heard about 'The Dark Side of Oz'.

Seamus bought a large black coffee, noticing for the first time, the prominent rainbows featured on the poster's art, before slipping into the dark, empty theatre.

Seamus came out of the art-house space nearly 2 hours later, his mind thoroughly blown. Pink Floyd had always been his favorite band to get high to; not *once* did he think about doing drugs. The Wizard of Oz was the only movie that he remembered watching with his mom, before she'd left. Seamus had been 4 years old. A toothless skull flashed through

His mind quickly returned to the movie. The guys in Floyd just *had* to be watching and sequencing the album to the movie in order for that shit to come together, like that...

Pondering the magical nature of what he'd just seen, Seamus thought long and hard upon that ticket was it just a coincidence that EL Cruz was only 13 miles north of Marshville? He'd asked the parole board to assign him an officer there. Marshville, not El Cruz. He'd been planning to return home. There were demons he needed to face there. Some bad men, too. But mainly just demons.

Seamus broke his own train of thought as he noticed a cute little hippie girl, wearing a multi-colored tie-dye shirt, go bouncing into an ice cream shop across the street. Suddenly, Seamus had a craving for some ice cream.

As he entered the Ice Cream Shoppe, the buxom hippie girl turned to Seamus and smiled. With the air-conditioning, it was apparent that she wasn't wearing a bra. She was wearing short, ragged little cut-off jean shorts. She was a short, curvy little thing. There was a word for girls like her, no matter where you came from. Trouble.

The soda jerk, a tongue-tied goon of a kid, stole her attention away. "Uh…Uhm, your… Uh, uhm…Your ice cream. Actually, it's er, uh…uhm—It's, uh, Rainbow sherbet, actually," He spastically sputtered out.

The hippie girl paid the soda jerk, taking a seat at a red and white striped table.

"I'll have what the ladies having." Seamus said, wincing. The soda jerk rolled his eyes. He scooped up 2 wimpy little scoops in a cup, placing a sugar cone upside-down, on top of the sherbert in the waxy cardboard bowl. As where hippie girl's sugar cone was placed at an artful angle, the cone on Seamus' bowl of sherbert sat perfectly upright, like a dunce cap. Shifting the cone off to an angle, Seamus asked the hippie girl if he could have a seat. Provocatively sucking on a pink spoon, hippie girl kicked out the red plastic chair that was sitting across from her.

Taking a seat, Seamus introduced himself. She seductively slurped the remaining sherbet off the tip of her spoon.

"Rainbow," the curvy hippie girl in the tie-dyed Grateful Dead shirt said, wiping her wavy chestnut and auburn locks away from her eyes. They were like green emeralds, and it was clearly obvious that she'd been crying. "And yes, that's my real name! Rainbow Sunshine Brighton," she added, with a sad little frown.

"Your name is Rainbow Brighton?" Seamus asked, breaking into a wide grin, "Like Rainbow Bright? The doll?"

"Yes, like Rainbow Fucking Bright, the Doll!" She snapped, "And yes, my parents smoked a lot of weed! And now I'm never, ever going to get my chance to get out of this little backwards hick town."

This outburst drew the soda jerk's full attention, who silently, sheepishly watched on while polishing his ice-cream scoop.

It didn't matter if her name was mud. Rainbow Sunshine Brighton was the type of girl that most men would follow like puppy dogs to the 4 corners of the Earth, and possibly even Hell itself. Seamus included.

"I think it's cute... No... Really." He said, keeping a straight face. "So...why don't you tell me what's really bothering you?"

"I lost something..."

Seamus thought of the found bus ticket, tucked inside his coat pocket. "It wouldn't happen to be a bus ticket, would it?"

"Oh my God, how did you know?" Rainbow Brighton blurted out. Seamus produced the ticket from his pocket. As he passed it across the table to Rainbow, the light once again hit the hologram, turning the corner of the ticket into a blazing aurora borealis of color.

"No way, dude!?" Rainbow shouted. "Way!" Seamus answered. For the next 15 minutes, Seamus and Rainbow sat eating sherbet, quickly becoming fast friends. When they had finished, Seamus O'Toole followed Rainbow Brighton to the Greyhound station, where, without reservation, without hesitation, he bought his own coach class ticket to EL Cruz...

The bus ride from Arcata to EL Cruz was a 12-hour trip. As the Greyhound pulled out of the terminal, neither Seamus nor his new muse, Rainbow, glanced out of the bus's windows. The place they were departing from, was a place they both wished to leave very far behind them, so they slept for a little while. It was hours into their trip that Rainbow, his muse, gave Seamus a brief rundown of her life story.

After Seamus had pointed out several holes in her story, Rainbow confessed to being a 17-year-old runaway. She'd bailed from a group home. Seamus felt his stomach lurch. After that, Seamus feigned sleep, until dreams eventually pushed all thoughts from his mind. Once the Sandman had taken possession of Seamus' dreams, he slept the fretful sleep of travelers.

It took Seamus a few moments to orient himself when he woke up. For a brief moment, he thought he was on a bus transporting him from jail to prison. Seamus looked out the window. It was dark out there, but he could see the ocean. A sign that read Moss Beach whizzed past his field of vision. The next sign came into view: Pescadero 22 miles, Davenport 38 miles, El Cruz 63 miles.

Seamus turned to Rainbow. She was sound asleep. He turned his gaze to the great Pacific Ocean. The next 63 miles soon became asphalt beneath the tires of the behemoth bus...

By the time they pulled into the EL Cruz Greyhound station, Rainbow had startled awake. She looked every bit the frightened kid she actually was. The bus station's glowing clock told them it was 4:15 in the morning, and all sorts of unsavory characters seemed to be trolling about; just out of reach of the glowing lights of the station. Rainbow and Seamus exited the bus, taking a seat on a cold, concrete bench. Rainbow snuggled up next to Seamus. He didn't push her away, enjoying the warmth...her softness... Within minutes, Rainbow fell fast asleep, while Seamus kept watch. The next few hours passed very slowly, as the morning chill crept into Seamus' bones.

With the morning came a magnificent light show, the sky fading from purple to violet, violet to magenta, magenta to orange, then eventually turning blue. People began to appear on the streets other than the nighttime weirdoes. Several bakeries and coffeehouses had opened, the aroma of their wares filling the air. Seamus roused Rainbow, suggesting coffee and a muffin, relishing his new found freedom. There were plenty of student types out and about; these were mixed in with a healthy sprinkling of professionals, along with a few local business owners. With Seamus looking youthful, and Rainbow mature beyond her age, they would easily pass as a college couple out for a stroll to get their morning coffee. The Greyhound station backed up to Oceana Avenue, the main drag of downtown EL Cruz. It was an open-air mall, providing several blocks of dining and shopping. Before long, Seamus and Rainbow found themselves at Pete's coffee house; large cups of steaming hot, rich, black coffee soon warming their hands. They both got pumpkin-ginger muffins, to go, where they had no trouble finding a bench on the street amongst the hustle and bustle of the early morning crowd. They ate their light breakfast while people watching, not saying much to one another.

In those early morning hours, Seamus had thought long and hard about the right thing to do. "Rainbow, you've got to go back home. I'm buying you a ticket when the bus station opens," After that he'd have about $170 left. Luckily, he'd been set up to stay in a halfway house down in Marshville, but not for a few more nights. He'd also been placed in a prisoner release work program. He'd be starting as an electrician making $22 an hour the following week. After living rough, Seamus figured he could get by on $170 for a few nights. So, that settled it, he was definitely buying Rainbow a one-way ticket home. The thought of seeing a sweet young thing like Rainbow Brighton go made his heart sink into his stomach. He was a changed man, though. A new man. Seamus O'Toole was a man who made good decisions. Seamus O'Toole was a man whose luck was turning... Round and round and round it goes, where it stops nobody knows — Rainbow Brighton dropped the final bombs, raining Daisy Cutters down on Seamus' parade. She was, in fact, only 16 years old; just turned. Rainbow hadn't actually run away from a group home, but from her parents' house. They were worried sick about her, and she had over 30 text messages to prove it. The last one said that the Humboldt Police had pinged her location, and they'd contacted El Cruz P.D.

Seamus felt his heart rise up to his throat. Nodding to himself, he felt like the man he was supposed to be. By 9 am, Seamus and Rainbow were the first people in line at the Greyhound station. Seamus plunked down $150 for Rainbow's return ticket to Humboldt County. Just before she stepped onto the rumbling Greyhound, Rainbow stepped up, giving Seamus a big hug. He did his best to keep it brotherly, as he felt her large breasts squish against his chest.

Stepping up onto the bus, he couldn't help but notice the curve of her bottom. He felt a tug on his heart and a stiffness in his groin... Seamus got himself under control, watching as the bus pulled away; Rainbow's hand splayed upon the window. He looked from her sad but smiling face to the station clock. It was a quarter 'til 10. The morning was still overcast. He could smell the sea-salty air.

Seamus strolled off in the direction of a sign pointing towards the beach. As a kid, he'd seen commercials for the El Cruz Beach Boardwalk. He'd always wanted to go, but his dad would never take him, even though it was only 13 miles away. He figured this was his chance to finally check it out, even if it was the off-season. It was mid-October. The fresh ocean air was like heaven after being locked up behind walls for seven years. Seamus couldn't help but smile. He felt as though he'd just dodged some sort of statutory-rape bullet. Not that they'd done anything inappropriate, or anything. He'd done the right thing. He'd been a man of principles... It was a Tuesday and Seamus couldn't check in to the halfway house until Saturday, sometime after noon. With the little bit of money in his pocket, Seamus considered trying to find a cheap motel and flopping in El Cruz for a few nights. If he could find a place for $40 a night, he'd have enough to stay for two nights, get some cheap grub, and still have enough for a bus ticket to Marshville *with* a few dollars to spare. El Cruz was already proving to be an interesting enough place; he figured he wouldn't need to spend much money on entertainment. Maybe just a beer or two. Booze had never really been Seamus' real problem. And 7 years in prison can make a man mighty thirsty for a beer. Or maybe even 2... Lost in thought, Seamus eventually found himself confronted with looming monstrosities, lurking vaguely in the morning's mist. It took him a moment or two to realize what it was he was looking at the quiet, enormous skeletons of the hibernating amusement rides It was the EL Cruz Beach Boardwalk, the attraction's silhouette's barely showing, through the creeping wall of misty fog.

Seamus decided to take a stroll along the deserted boardwalk. Even though the rides weren't operating, the boardwalk itself was open year round. Today was a ghost-town. The marine layer was so thick, he couldn't even see the ocean. He could hear it, and smell it, though. Even taste it. Seamus found the steady rhythmic sound of the breaking waves, to be incredibly soothing. If he could find a cheap motel that he could hear the pounding of the surf from, he would definitely stay in EL Cruz for the next few nights. After walking the boardwalk's entire length, Seamus found himself exiting out onto a street that appeared to be pretty run down. Both sides of the street were filled with grubby little beach cottages, built in little courtyards. Seamus struck off towards one of these.

The small, dented metallic sign, paint peeling, announced: Squid Head's Court. There were six small little cottages arranged in a U-shape, around a dried up swimming pool. The seventh cottage was thrust out a bit from the U-shape, with a sign on the door that said: Office. Seamus entered the seventh cottage, to the tinkling of tiny bells; the sound of which seemed to nearly put Seamus into a kind of trance state. He heard footsteps approaching from the back rooms. A not very pleasant smell proceeded the back room's occupant. Seamus hoped his face remained neutral as the occupant, who Seamus assumed was the manager, came waddling up to the registration desk. The woman was very short but also very large. Her face was painted like Cleopatra, or, perhaps Nefertiti. Her hair was cut at an angle following her jaw line; it was dyed turquoise, matching her eyeshadow. She was smoking a meerschaum pipe, carved like some sort of an octopus, the fragrant smell of marijuana filling the room. She wore a muumuu that looked like it had come from Hilo Hattie's; or perhaps Mrs. Roper's closet. Like her hair and her eyeshadow, it was also a dazzling turquoise color. Where her arms and legs were bear, the pale folds of her white, vein-decorated flesh reminded Seamus of the Michelin man.

"You have any Vacancy's, Ma'am?" He asked, putting on the charm. "And if so, what's your rate for 3 nights?" Seamus gave her his best smile.

"I usually rent by the week," she croaked, giving Seamus a horrifying plastic grin, with pipe clenched between teeth. "It just so happens, though, we had a vacancy just last night. Bungalow number three. And I *guess* I could bend the rules, for a sweet little morsel like you. I'll give it to you, for say, 90 bucks. And that's cash. What do you say, Buster?" Seamus couldn't get the cash out fast enough. The room was cheaper than he thought. That gave him a little extra spending money for his impromptu vacation. He was going to go and have a nice dinner at a Mexican food restaurant tonight. The large, squat lady handed Seamus the key to bungalow 3, adding, "If you get lonely give me holler. And if you see something weird, and go running off in the night, don't expect your money back!" Seamus thanked Squat Lady, and then hurried off to bungalow 3. He'd felt like he was getting a contact high and he couldn't have that. There'd be a drug test at his P.O.'s.

Opening the door to bungalow 3, the first thing Seamus noticed was the reek of cigarette smoke. He quickly opened the windows which, luckily, had screens on them. He could hear the steady rhythm of the surf. He could smell the salty air of the sea. Good enough. Seamus flopped himself down on the mattress, 100 bed springs, maybe more, squealing in protest. Most people would probably consider it an uncomfortable bed, but it was more comfortable than the bed he'd slept on in prison; and it beat the hell out of any sidewalk he'd *ever* slept on, or bush he'd ever woke up under, for that matter. After fitful sleep, at best, over the last 2 nights, *and* acting as Rainbow's sentinel through the wee hours of the morning, Seamus drifted off into the land of peaceful sleep; to the sound of the constant sea...

II

And it was that same pounding surf that Seamus awoke to each time a wave would break upon the shore, an immense pain would ripple from his temples through his brain. He didn't know how long he had slept, but the light outside was gray and dull. It was still too bright for Seamus. His tongue swollen and thick; It felt like hot coals had been placed in his belly. His stomach boiled, as though some alien beast were ready to burst forth, screeching and howling, from within. Fluid filled his gorge—

Quickly rising to his feet, Seamus hobbled to the bathroom, where he vomited first in the sink; then in the toilet bowl. When he was through he washed the sink, then rinsed his face, before returning to the squeaky bed. Like quick cuts from a movie, the previous night came flashing back to Seamus...

After waking from his nap, which he could only assume had been last night, he'd been hungry, and gone in search of the Mexican food dinner he'd promised himself. He'd walked back into town, finding a pretty nice-looking sit-down place. Not some quick taqueria. After enjoying a bowl of chips and salsa with a Tecate, his first beer in 7 years, Seamus decided on a classic number 1 combination plate. Chicken taco, cheese enchilada, with rice and beans. He'd ordered a second beer with dinner. Then a third, *after* dinner, followed by a shot of tequila. No. Make that *2* tequilas. Dinner and his bar tab had come to $34. He'd left $40 on the table. That was just *before* he'd become belligerent; just *before* he was thrown out!

Seamus shuddered, as he vaguely remembered showing the cute Latina waitress his tattoo, before being tossed out of the place on to his ass. He quickly decided he'd have to remove that God-damned tattoo.

After about an hour, Seamus got up and vomited in the toilet again; half from the alcohol, half from the fact that he'd spent nearly half of his remaining money on last night's celebration. He'd have to be careful tonight. No beers. *Definitely* no tequilas. Eventually, the sound of the throbbing ocean merged with the throbbing of his headache, becoming one constant throb. The dirty gray light slowly slipped away, to a darker shade of slate.

It was close to 6 o'clock in the evening when Seamus finally startled awake. For a brief moment, he thought of a skull found in a construction-site dumpster when he was 4; And, of a monstrous cartoon leprechaun, but, the thought soon passed, as it always did... The sleep had done him well. He felt much, much, better. After a quick shower, Seamus grabbed his coat, walking into town on foot. Before he'd left, he'd put one of his last two $20 bills in the pages of what passed as a Bible; though it was a Bible of no religion Seamus had ever heard of, The Order of Xushathula, that had been tucked in the back of the nightstand's drawer...

Once again Seamus awoke to the sound of pounding surf, along with the noise of his own chattering teeth. It felt as though the lumpy mattress was trying its hardest to swallow him whole; it was far more uncomfortable than he remembered it being the previous night. Shivering, he scrambled about for the threadbare blanket, before opening his eyes. He was startled into a sitting position, the events of last night unfolding in his brain. He panicked, looking this way and that

After splurging the night before, Seamus had promised himself he would take it easy. And he did. In fact, after strolling around downtown EL Cruz for a few hours, Seamus had stopped by a convenience store to grab a few snacks; cheesy peanut butter crackers, a beef stick, and a 16 ounce can of cola. He'd only spent $4.75, of the $20 he'd brought with him. After that, he'd walked back to his run-down mini bungalow, at the Squid Head's Court.

Seamus had happily munched down his snacks, washing them down with his soda, while watching the small black-and-white TV; it only received 3 channels, so his options were limited. He left it on the channel showing reruns of Mama's Family and Benson. Bored out of his gourd, he eventually dozed off amongst the wreckage of his makeshift convenience store dinner, and antiquated sit-coms.

It must've been sometime after midnight that Seamus was startled awake, by a loud knocking on the bungalow's door. Jumping out of bed, he quickly inquired, voice an octave deeper, "Who's there?"

"Landlady." A voice croaked, the voice of Squat Lady, from the office, "Could you open up?"

A wave of confusion washed over Seamus. But he recognized Squat Lady's voice; that *was* her. He opened the door, to be greeted with the pungent waft of marijuana smoke, puffing like a chimney, from her carved meerschaum pipe. The whites of her eyes were blood red. Not just blood-shot. The whites were completely red, contrasting her blue-green irises.

"Well, can I come in?" She wheezed, smoke pouring from her mouth.

"What's this all about?"

"There are *some* things on this earth that are *not* to be questioned, boy. Besides, whose house are you in?" Squat Lady bum rushed Seamus, driving him to the back wall of the cottage. He couldn't believe that someone with such bulk could move so fast. There was something inhuman in the way that she moved.

"You *are* a sweet little morsel, *aren't* you?" Smoke billowed from her nostrils, spaced too wide; smoke plumed from her open mouth, filled with teeth too sharp. Seamus didn't know how to answer. The smell of sardines seemed to emit from her every pore.

Suddenly, her blood red eyes rolled back into her head, blue-green irises gone, and seemed to be lit from behind; glowing! What Seamus had taken to be her pendulous breasts, her flabby tummy, began writhing beneath her muumuu. Squat Lady lifted that muumuu, exposing her naughty bits. Her flesh was a ruined mass of pus-filled boils; nubs and nubbins; along with small, wiggling tentacles, that reminded Seamus of earthworms. There was a large lamprey-like mouth, filled with triangular teeth, opening and closing where a belly button should have been. Things that looked like crab legs, grasped at thin air from between her thighs.

Luckily, Seamus had fallen asleep fully dressed, shoes and all. He feigned one direction, then bolted the other, moving past the horrifying creature, hurrying out the door of bungalow number 3. The neighbors took little to no notice, this being a regular occurrence that happens at Squid Head's Court, once or twice a week. Seamus ran off, yelling in the night. He'd left his $20 bill in that book that looked like a Bible that wasn't a bible, but he *did* have the mind to grab his coat from the chair by the door.

Seamus had run all the way back down to the boardwalk, then down to the beach, where he had sat until shock and exhaustion overtook him.

Seamus scrambled around in the sand, until he clutched his coat, pulling it back on like a blanket. He wouldn't be going back for that $20. No way. No way in Hell. Seamus wiped the morning drizzle from his face pulling his coat a little bit higher to cover his head. Somehow, he dozed back off.

At least for a little while; The flow of the St. Lorenzo River, letting out into the grandeur of the Pacific Ocean, the mist letting up and turning to a dirty blue sky. Here and there, the cry of a gull piercing all the way through, invading into Seamus' sleeping subconscious. The shore break had gone from pounding to lapping. It was all so very soothing.

A tattoo-beat tapped Seamus in his ribs, startling him out of his slumber. There was a shrill squawking in his ears. He cursed the seagulls, then the seagulls began talking back.

"Hey buddy, you can't be sleeping here," the squawking said. A tattoo-beat on the other side of his ribcage; Then, a different squawking seagull's voice.

"Come on. Get up!"

Seamus opened his eyes, focusing on 2 park rangers, clad in turd brown uniforms. They both wore short-sleeved button up work-shirts, along with short dolphin-shorts. Judging by the matching helmets they were carrying under their arms, these guys must've been bicycle patrol.

"Relax," Seamus says, relieved they're not actually cops, "I'm just enjoying a day at the beach." Seamus looked up and down the long stretch of sand; from river-mouth to wharf. With the exception of the seagulls, Seamus seemed to be the only one enjoying a day by the shore, or at least *pretending* to be. It seemed that bike patrol knew how to spot a down-and-outer when they saw one.

"Don't tell me to relax!" Park Ranger Number 2 told Seamus, "If you're enjoying the day at the beach, then where's your bag? Your towel?"

"Your cooler, your trunks, your umbrella?" Park Ranger Number 1 cut off Park Ranger Number 2. It definitely wasn't the type of day that someone would just put on swim trunks and go diving into the ocean.

"We saw you here over 2 hours ago. In the same spot! Look, you've got 2 choices," Number 2 regained control over the conversation, "I can either give you a ticket for loitering, and that's $125 fine..." Number 2 let it linger, a drawn-out pause for dramatic effect.

"That seems like a lot of money for a guy like you." Number 1 seized the opportunity to chime in. Park Ranger Number 2 shot Park Ranger Number 1 daggers over his cheap, mirrored, gas-station sunglasses.

"Or," Number 2 continued, asserting his authority over the situation, again, "you can pay the $10-day use fee. Directly to me."

"This is a public beach. There's no day use fee." Seamus snorted his reply.

"For scumbags like you there are!" Number 1 piped up, and chimed in.

"Shut it!" Number 2 snapped at Number 1, then turned his back on Seamus, quickly pulling something from his leather fanny-pack. He held up his ticket book, waving it in Seamus' face, his own face beet-red, "I have full power and authority to use this. I can, and will, write you a ticket. That puts you in front of a judge, pal! By the look of those tattoos, you probably don't want to go up in front of a judge. $10-day use fee, or I write you a fine for loitering. I can make up some counts, too, if you can't pay up," The smug look on Number 2's face said he didn't think Seamus had a snowball's chance of producing that 10 spot.

If this had been the old Seamus O'Toole, high on a cocktail of drugs fueled with booze, he might've bit the patrolman's nose and lips off. It wouldn't have been the first time. If there was one thing Seamus had been in his previous life, Seamus had been tough. But that was the past, luckily, for Park Ranger Number 2. Seamus dug into his pocket, pulling out the bills folded up within. He was a new man. A changed man. He peeled the $10 bill away from the $5 bill, handing it to Park Ranger Number 2. Park Ranger Number 2 looked furious. He eyeballed the $5 bill that Seamus held in his other hand.

"Oh I'm sorry! Did I say the day use was $10? It's actually a $15 fee," Number 2 said putting on a patronizing smile that Seamus wanted to punch. With an exhale, Seamus stacked the 2 bills together, handing them to Number 2. He'd be a good man...

As cool as he could, Seamus said, "Here you go."

Park Ranger Number 2 snatched the bills out of his hands, stuffing them into the pocket of his own short shorts, "The beach is closed today! As of now! Got it friend?!" Number 2 let his mirrored glasses slide down his nose, just a bit, so that he could give Seamus a stern look over the top of them. Total asshole...

"Yeah I got it." Seamus answered the walking, talking, piece of shit—

The 2 park rangers turned and walked off towards the wharf. After about 50 steps in the sand, they retrieved their bikes, which had been hidden in the dip of a small sand-dune. The rangers walked their mountain bikes down to the waterline, where they mounted their cycles, before peddling off towards the wharf, on the hard packed sand.

'Butt-fucks!' Seamus thought, watching them ride away. He got up, dusted the sand off of himself and began following in the park rangers' footsteps. Instead of walking towards the ocean though, he turned up towards the seawall. His legs burned by the time he hit the stairwell that lead him up to the street. Thankfully the park rangers had disappeared.

Seamus struck off towards the wharf, walking along the sidewalk. Once he'd reached the wharf, he had turned inland on 1st Street, then eventually walked back up to Oceana Avenue. He suddenly walked into a cloud that smelled of sizzling meat, spicy and aromatic. His stomach savagely growled. The sky was just beginning to lose light, turning from late noon to early evening as Seamus walked past The Gyro House; the *obvious* source of that delicious, mouth-watering aroma. Again his stomach rumbled. And here he was, without a dollar to his name; without a pot to piss in.

Seamus had tried doing the right thing; tried to be a changed man; tried to be a new man; tried to be a good man. And look where all that had landed him.

As Seamus walked past The Gyro House, he stopped short as he noticed the park rangers' bicycles propped up outside the eatery. The next thing Seamus observed, a sign. It read: Gyro Special: Gyro, French fries and a fountain drink, $7.50. It was Seamus' last observation, though, that nearly drove him completely mad. Through the window Seamus saw the rangers wolfing down mammoth gyros; grubbing on enormous baskets of fries, already half devoured; sucking down large sodas, sweating with icy condensation.

Seamus was fuming, ready to go inside and give those 2 wanna-be pigs a piece of his fuckin' mind. He was hungry, and those 2 butt-fucks were eating food that he'd paid for. He'd paid for it dearly! And then, just as Seamus was reaching for the door handle of the Gyro House, something up the street caught his attention, like a fishing lure—

A flash of rainbow color—

And then it was gone; but, no! There it was again! A sign, blinking the spectrum of the rainbow; it read: Beer $1, before winking off again.

At that same moment; Seamus was aware of a weight, his old nylon wallet, forgotten, there in his back pocket. He reached back, pulling it out, separating the Velcro. He opened the wallet and there they were the $2 he'd had on his person when he'd been arrested, all those years ago.

Now, from the Irish-American standpoint, beer *technically* was food. Of a sort. Seamus decided to forget about the 2 turkeys in the Gyro shop and focused on the $2 in his old nylon wallet. Suddenly, Seamus was mighty thirsty, again.

As Seamus walked towards the flashing rainbow beer sign, he had a quick flashback to when his life had spiraled out of control. Seamus envisioned himself a 12 pack deep, finished off with half a dozen shots of whiskey. This was just before he'd become homeless, of course. At 21, he'd usually smoke a little crack *before* hitting the bars, do a little cocaine while *at* the bars, and then see where the night would take him from there. In those years, between 21 and 23, there were many of those nights that took him to strange, dark, places. He shook his head, trying to shake off the memories. Seamus reasoned with himself that the $2 wasn't enough to do any real damage; besides, maybe he'd only have one beer, just to prove to himself that he could. All though, he *was* thirsty...

Seamus finally came to the entrance of the club. The place, according to the neon purple sign, was called 'Koda. A different sign, the rainbow sign, flashed: Beer $1. It winked out again. Seamus, feeling like he had sand in his throat, feeling like he could die of thirst, grabbed the door handle, swinging it open. Upon entering, he was greeted by a staircase, which led to the upper floors. Seamus began walking up the wide wooden stairs, which groaned under his weight with each step. Seamus soon came out on the 2nd floor.

It was a small gallery space, painted black and purple. Mostly black, though. The floors and ceilings, likewise, were painted black. White, full body casts, of multi-limbed humanoids that were displaying curious combinations of male/female sex parts, all in some various form of self-pleasuring hung from the walls, lit in lurid neon black lights. The faces of all the sculptures were featureless, with the exception of hollowed out eye sockets. The eye sockets were each lit with small, green neon lights, set in tight clusters, 3 in each eye. Looking at these strange homoerotic statues on the walls, Seamus strongly considered turning on a heel, walking down those creaky stairs, and out into the wholesome, early evening air. But his thirst was *strong*. Looking around, Seamus saw the next stairwell, leading up to the next floor. As soon as he'd opened the door, Seamus heard the muffled thump of pumping disco music. He continued up the stairs, in search of a dollar beer. But definitely just one. The art gallery had made up his mind for him on that one.

Seamus came up to the 3rd floor landing, thumping bass much, much louder now. Just up ahead were a pair of double doors with round portholes, head high, set in the center of each door. The doors were padded black leather, the upholstered buttons forming diamond patterns. As Seamus reached for one of the 2 handles, he'd noticed that they were sculpted like winged pixies. He grabbed one of the nude sprites, peering through the porthole. The entire room was painted black like the gallery below, lit only by twinkle lights strung across the ceiling, along with a flood of neon purple black lights washing down the wall behind the bar. Seamus could only make out the silhouettes of the patrons inside; what appeared to be a few ink blobs sitting at different tables, and 2 more behind the bar.

Seamus swung the door open, the treble joining the bass as the music sprang to life. He vaguely recognized the song; a band called Depeche Mode, he thought, talking about Jesus. Seamus could feel all eyes inside the place focus on him, the moment he'd stepped foot into the bar. As he made his final approach, the long empty bar seemed to stretch off further into space than it should have, some kind of forced perspective; a very strange optical illusion. Everything was lit in eerie violet light.

The first bartender was a petite girl, that wouldn't have been out of place in a 1940s men magazine; Or, sitting on the side of a World War II bomber plane. She was brunette, with bangs, hair pulled into a high ponytail. Seamus couldn't help but notice her thigh-high stockings through the slit of her skirt. The skin of her thigh was creamy and pale. Little Seamus noticed, too! She paid Seamus no heed at all.

The other bartender, was tall and burly, barrel chested, and wearing overalls; thick forearms covered in traditional Americana tattoos; a red goatee, trimmed in a style known as a Van Dyke, sprouted from her chin; she wore a red handkerchief on her head; a butch Rosie the riveter. She was the one who'd barked at Seamus.

"What do you want?! Ladies night starts in 45 minutes. Ladies only! Catch my drift, creep?" Her voice was rough and tumble, gruff. Definitely the voice of at least a pack-a-day smoker. She wore a grill, made of faux-gold, 'Muff-Diver' spelled out in cubic zirconium, across her teeth.

"I saw the dollar beer sign flashing outside. Does that go for anything? Do you have anything dark, a stout, maybe?"

Butch Rosie started laughing, which quickly turned to a bout of smoker's cough. A large figure came crashing through the double doors.

"Cur's only...for," Butch Rosie looked back at a black-light lit clock, it read 6:13. "You've got another 17 minutes. You want one?" The look on her face told Seamus he should say no. The lumbering, dark figure, approached the bar. Seamus couldn't *stand* Cur's; a cheap, cheap, pilsner that made Pabst or Olympia seem pretty classy by comparison. If the name didn't say it, the Brown can, with a mutt that looked like it was frozen in mid-retch, said it all. Fucking thing looked like it should be euthanized.

Seamus refused to leave, like that beat dog on the can, whimpering with his tail tucked between his legs, "Yeah, I'll have one of those." He told Butch Rosie, a defiant twinkle in his eye.

"All right, all right!" Butch Rosie barked, storming off to the far side of the bar.

A raspy voice asked, "Can ye turn the radio down now, Lassie," the thick Irish brogue was more commanding, rather than requesting. As if hypnotized, the World War II bomber pinup, walked over to the stereo console, and turned it off.

"Hey, what do you think you're doing?!" Butch Rosie yelled at World War II bomber pinup.

"This doesn't concern ye," the cheese-grater-like voice said. Seamus turned to get a look at the stranger, as Butch Rosie fell silent and resumed filling the pint that Seamus had ordered. The stranger was tall! 6'6", maybe 6'7"; he was brawny in the chest and narrow in the waist, the man given even *more* mass by the moss green trench-coat that he wore; his coat weathered, beaten, threadbare beyond belief. Around his neck, poking through his wiry black beard, he wore a necklace of animal's bones; a bird skull hung from the center like a pendent. A bright gleaming stone, a stone of shifting colors, was strung between each bone, on either side. The man's hair was as wild as his beard, although it was greasier; worn long, and slicked straight back. Perched atop his head, he wore a bent, crumpled, top hat; hatband covered in all sorts of trinkets, and bric-a-brac. Out of a dozen black barstools, the looming stranger decided to take the one *right* next to Seamus, pulling it away from the bar, with a fingernails-on-chalkboard screech. Seamus winced. The large, weird stranger, sat heavily upon the sturdy stool, which squealed in protest under the load.

The stranger began sniffing the air around Seamus. The stranger began to grin, his face that of a leering gargoyle's wrought from living flesh.

"What are you doing?" Seamus turned on the weird character. Probably some kind of pervert, he guessed.

"I can smell yer desperation, laddie," the Irish weirdo winked at Seamus. A flash of lightning blue.

"Calm down laddie, were two of a kind, we are," the stranger turned and stared at Seamus, "you and I."

Seamus had a difficult time pealing his eyes away from the stranger's gaze; Seamus felt he'd lost the contest of wills, when he finally broke contact, looking away from those malamute eyes; eyes the color of blue glacial ice. Or heaven sent lightning. The stranger continued:

"See, I've been a wee bit down on me luck as of late. Down to me last twenty spot," the weird man reached out to shake hands with Seamus. Seamus couldn't help but notice the stranger's spidery fingers; they seemed unnaturally long. Too long—

Against his better judgment Seamus reached out, returning the stranger's handshake. The stranger grabbed Seamus by the wrist, in an old-fashioned grasp, his creepy long fingers nearly reaching Seamus' elbow. The stranger's spider fingers caressed him; tickling him there.

Seamus sensed a great power within the weird man; as if the stranger could tear his arm from his body, with one massive pull.

"The name's Gerald John, but me friends do call me Gerry John," The raspy voiced stranger announced. He'd pronounced Gerry like Jerry, "and ye?"

"Seamus. Seamus O'Toole." Seamus had automatically answered, no doubt the result of all those years behind bars. He'd almost given him his penal code number, too. "You're doin' better than me. I'm down to my last dollar.

"Well, are ye down for a game o' chance, young Seamus?" Gerry John reached into the folds of his voluminous overcoat, quickly pulling something out, only to reveal 3 cups, and—what appeared to be—a large Navy bean. "You do believe in chance, Seamus, don't'cha? Luck?" Upon closer inspection, Seamus thought the cups almost looked like they could have been the cranial caps of small children, probably made of resin (it had to be, right?); the bean, appeared to be some sort of larva, or cocoon, unlike anything Seamus had ever seen. He was pretty damn sure that he saw something move inside the semi-opaque husk, backlit in the violet black light glow of 'Koda, if only for a brief moment.

Seamus had won a lot of smokes in the pen, playing this very game, the shell game, on the prison-yard. He usually gave them away to the guys that he hung around with, another part of the deal to keep from getting ass-fucked in the showers. Seamus wondered what this dude Gerry John's *real* story was. Butch Rosie plunked the pint of Cur's down, hard, in front of Seamus before plodding off. Foam came erupting out of the top of his glass.

"What are the stakes?" Seamus asked.

"How a 'bout a pint? Ye'll buy me a pint if I win. If I lose, I'll give ye me last twenty dollars. Is it a deal?"

Seamus hesitated, a weird feeling filling his gut. He wondered if that was what *luck* actually felt like? 'No,' Seamus thought, 'This isn't luck, and this isn't chance. This is skill. I've won this game. Won it a thousand times.'

"All right, let's play, then," Seamus said to Gerry John.

"Yes, let's," Gerry John replied, lifting the middle cup (skullcap?), and flicked the bean (larva?) beneath it, dropping the cup (skullcap?) to the bar top, "Round and round and round it goes, where it stops nobody knows!" Gerry John's spider-like fingers shuffled the cups, impossibly fast, before suddenly coming to an abrupt halt. Seamus listened more than watched, but he did that, too. It was the sound of the bean, or whatever object that was being used in its place, bouncing off the inside of the cup, that would usually give its location away. There was no sound. None. This guy was good. Really good...

Seamus couldn't believe it, but he'd lost track of the bean (larva?). He pointed to the cup (skullcap?) to the left. Gerry John turned the cup (skullcap?) over.

Nothing. Nada. Zip... Gerry John began to chuckle, sounding like some ancient engine, trying to kick over. "Looks like ye owe me a cold one, laddie," Gerry John winked a piercing blue eye at Seamus. "Hey lassie, make it one more o' what the gent here's drinkin'," he called out to Butch Rosie. For only the briefest of moments, she looked like she wanted to tell him to go and shove it where the sun doesn't shine, and perhaps not even in such an eloquent way. Gerry John wiggled his spidery fingers at Butch Rosie and growled, "Now!" Like Fagan from 'Oliver Twist'.

Butch Rosie's face went slack as she began pouring a pint of Cur's for Gerry John. There was a smell emanating from Gerry John, the smell of boiling corned beef, and cabbage. Seamus felt the hairs on the back of his neck stand on end, tingling with electricity.

Butch Rosie came stomping back as if she were a lobotomy patient, dropping the pint down in front of Gerry John, foaming beer sloshing over the rim. In an instant all her surliness returned. "That'll be a dollar!" Gerry John tilted his head in Seamus' direction to indicate he'd be the one picking up the tab. "Two dollars, then! Well?" Butch Rosie barked. Seamus reached into his back pocket, fishing out his nylon wallet, tearing open the Velcro, and pulling out his last two dollars on earth. With a deep sigh, he gently tossed them on to the bar top. Gerry John seemed to gulp at the air, as if trying to swallow Seamus' exhaled hopelessness.

Gerry John slapped Seamus on the back, licking his lips. Gerry John raised his pint, "Ye may be broke, but yer still just a wee laddie, you are. Let's drink to our health. Too Seamus O'Toole and Gerald John, may the sun always be at our backs, and the wind forever on our faces," Gerry John chuckled, "or is it the other way 'round? Doesn't really matter, it's all a bunch of malarkey! Now I'll drink to that!"

Seamus and Gerry John clinked glasses and drank. Gerry John finished his pint in a single gulp. The strange man let out a sigh of satisfaction, then wiped his mouth with the back of his hand. Gerry John's face became a mask of mischievous glee.

"Hey, laddie," his voice thick with Ireland, "whad'd'ya'say we play a 'nother round o' the cups?"

Gerry John tilted his head in the direction of the cups (skullcap's?).

"I don't have anything left to bet with." Seamus answered.

"Oh, there's plenty o' things a man can bet with. Look at me, by all accounts down and out, but, I," Gerry John reached inside his jacket, his pale, too-long fingers darting in and out in a flash; he held something clenched in his hand, "I have this. Me last twenty dollars. If you win," Gerry John's spidery fingers began wiggling up and down, Seamus caught something briefly flashing, appearing to vibrate across Gerry John's knuckles. In the next moment, the vibrating hand seemed to slow down, dramatically so, and Seamus saw the flashing object was a golden coin. It continued tumbling over Gerry John's knuckles, over and over, back and forth.

'Could that *actually* be a twenty-dollar gold piece?' Seamus thought. Then it hit him. Seamus realized he must be in the middle of a street performance, or some kind of gothic magic show, of sorts... His eyes fixed on the golden coin. The gold seemed a little *too* golden, a little *too* bright. It seemed, to Seamus, like maybe a chocolate covered coin. He figured a little bit of chocolate might taste pretty good right about now. "And if I lose?" He asked Gerry John, momentarily caught up in the strange man's parlor tricks.

"Well let's see? What's a man like ye got left to lose? Luck o' the Irish perhaps?" Gerry John asked inquisitively, "Nah, ye've never had any of that, anyway." He spits at the ground. The coin continued to dance over Gerry John's knuckles, almost impossibly so. In fact, everything in the disturbing purple light of 'Koda, seemed as though it had slowed down. Like molasses. Thick and syrupy, "Or, how about yer firstborn child? No, no, I have a friend, he's a *nasty* little fellow, and that's *his* thing, it is."

Gerry John smiled, his mouth becoming a rictus grin, his teeth jagged and uneven. Seamus had heard that people from the United Kingdom could have some *pretty* fucked up teeth, but Gerry John's seemed worse than normal; almost animalistic. "I know," the large, strange man turned his palm upwards, snatching the golden coin out of the air. He quickly pocketed the golden coin, shoving it into his tattered coat, "how about yer *soul*? Not now, of course, but when you're done with it! That could be tomorrow, or twenty, or fifty years from now."

Seamus took a sip off his pint, before placing it back on the bar. His soul?

Seamus decided to play along, seeing no harm in losing something that he didn't *really* believe even existed, anyway. Plus, this was *still* a game he'd won 1000 times. He could do this. And he couldn't wait to call out Gerry John on the $20 bet when he ended up winning that chocolate coin. Then again, Gerry John was big and broad, some might even say giant. Maybe he wouldn't call him out, after all. He'd eat the chocolate coin in front of him though, yeah, that would show him. And no, that's not some kind of weird sex act. At least not that I *know* of...

"You're on!" Seamus declared. For some reason, Seamus felt as though he'd just made a deal with the Devil. Satan. Lucifer. Beelzeb—you get the drift.

"All righty then, young Seamus," Gerry John said, placing the bean (larva?) beneath the center cup (skullcap?), "round and round and round it goes," Gerry John's hands became a blur, once again moving far too fast for Seamus to have any idea where the bean (larva?) may have actually been, "where it stops nobody knows!" Gerry John's hands spun yet even impossibly faster; a strange notion came to Seamus, the thought being that if he were to take his eyes off of the game, to look at the clock, he would somehow see the hands moving at an accelerated speed. He didn't take his eyes off the game, though. Suddenly Gerry John stopped.

Seamus didn't have even the slightest where the bean (larva?) had ended up. Once again, no lingering sound, to give up the bean's (larvae's?) hiding place. Seamus knew this game, knew most of its tricks. With some small degree of confidence, he pointed to the center cup (skullcap?). Sometimes, a crafty player wouldn't move the bean at all. They'd just let it sit there. Maybe—

Gerry John slowly lifted the cup (skullcap?) that Seamus had pointed to, careful to lift it away from Seamus' field of vision, as if he himself weren't sure of where the bean (larva?) had actually come to rest. A look of great disappointment came over Gerry John's face, causing Seamus to smile.

Gerry John lifted the cup (skullcap?), revealing an empty space beneath. Gerry John grinned a wicked grin, "Looks like what's yer's is mine, aye laddie?" The strange man seemed to gloat. Seamus made note that he didn't feel any different, despite having just lost his soul. Gerry John continued, "It wouldn't be gentlemanly of me not to offer ye one more chance, now would it?" He looked hostile.

Seamus had no idea where Gerry John was going with all of this. Gerry John gathered up the cups (skullcaps?) and the bean (larva?), shoving them into the folds of his coat. Once again, Gerry John's hand came darting out of his coat like a blur. He opened up his hand, palm up, the bright flash of gold once again in the palm of his hand. This time, Seamus saw the coin was a Saint-Gaudens, a coin that he knew was worth quite a bit of money. Gerry John continued his proposition:

"I have to make this enticing for ye, I do, because *now* ye're a man with nothing left to lose, but perhaps ye've still something to regain. I'll tell ye what, a game of pure chance. A simple coin toss. Ye call it. If ye win, I'll give ye back yer soul, and on top of it all, I'll grant ye three wishes. How about that?"

Seamus replied, "And if I lose?" Gerry John slid a single too-long finger, across his own throat. Seamus didn't know if that meant it was the end of the game, or Game Over.

This Gerry John character was one weird fellow.

"What the hell, let's do this," Seamus picked up his pint, finishing it off, semi-slamming the empty glass back down on the bar.

"That a boy!" Gerry John winked at him. "All right Seamus, are ye ready, then?" Seamus nodded his head in affirmation. Gerry John let loose his cocked thumb, releasing a golden flash up, up, and away; off into local orbit.

"Heads!" Seamus shouted, caught up in the moment. The coin flipped even higher yet, before reaching its zenith; the ceiling seemed impossibly tall. Then, the coin seemed to hover in midair longer than physically possible, before beginning its tumbling descent downwards. The coin clicked down on to the bar, as if drawn by some magnetic force. The coin was heads. He'd won a game of chance; a toss of luck...

Seamus let out his held breath, in a long windy sigh. For some strange reason, he suddenly felt relieved; even though he hadn't really felt anything tangible. And the 3 wishes? What in the hell was that all about?

Seamus looked around the bar. Everything seemed to be moving syrupy slow; he wondered if Gerry John had slipped something into his drink. Other than the weird time distortion, though, Seamus felt fine. Seamus eyeballed Gerry John, as the strange giant man picked up the coin, his last $20, and jammed it back into his coat. "Well young Seamus," Gerry John broke the momentary silence, "it appears I owe ye some wishes, now doesn't it. Well?"

A thought struck Seamus. He'd call out the shyster on his shenanigans. "All right, Gerry John," Seamus rubbed his chin pretending to think hard, "I've got it! My first wish... is for your last twenty dollars. How about that?" Seamus assumed that this was where the two of them would be parting ways.

"As you wish," Gerry John reached into his pocket, withdrew his hand, holding his clenched fist, palm down towards Seamus. Seamus reached an empty hand out towards Gerry John's. Gerry John opened his clenched fist; the coin's cool weight settled into the palm of Seamus' hand. "That was a good wish, fairly modest as far as wishes go." Gerry John told Seamus.

Seamus was gob-stopped. He studied the coin, which *was* a genuine Saint-Gaudens. It seems the one beer had given him an instant buzz; Seamus became giddy one instant, and in the next, he was wondering what Gerry John's *real* agenda could be. "You're actually going to let me keep this coin? Your last twenty dollars?"

"Aye, it's yer wish. There are certain contracts I'm bound to. Promises I have to keep. Besides, when I'd said it was me last twenty dollars, I meant for the night. I've got more of those coins than I know what to do with. So many, I couldn't spend them in two human lifetimes. Often times, I trade them to people...I'll trade 'em one of me coins for one of their bills. Paper money's just so much easier to spend these days. Not to mention carry around!"

The wheels inside Seamus' head began cranking away; he'd heard stories on the news, about eccentric millionaires spending fortunes on strange little philanthropic acts. He wondered if Gerry John was one of *those* types. The man was certainly eccentric enough. He almost seemed to have no idea of the true value of the coins that he said he'd so casually traded away; and he certainly seemed willing to grant these wishes that Seamus had supposedly won, bound by some kind of duty-driven honor; wishes won on a coin toss that Seamus took to be more a game of metaphor than a game of actuality.

"All right, Gerry John," Seamus thought about it, then scaled it back a bit; he didn't want to seem greedy, "for my second wish I want twenty more these coins," Seamus figured he'd pawn them one by one, spread out over time, so as not to draw any unwanted attention to himself. Seamus didn't realize, that as a felon, he wouldn't be able to pawn jack-shit.

"I can do that. Another sensible wish," Gerry John told Seamus, "but ye'll have to come back to me house with me, there's a bit o' work to be done in order to get at those coins."

Seamus became suspicious, wondering if this was how Gerry John lured unwitting conquests back to whatever sex-lair he'd crawled out from.

"I promise, no funny business," Gerry John told Seamus as though reading his mind, "I assure ye. I'm a married man, with a wife at home. It's just that the coins are buried in me backyard. And even though I may look hale 'n hearty, I'm no spring chicken."

As if on cue, Butch Rosie came stomping up, confronting first Gerry John, "All right! Times up, time for you to take your swingin' dick, and get the hell out of here!", Then turning on Seamus, "And even though you don't look like you have much of a dick to swing, it's time for you to beat it, too."

Again, a Broadway musical couldn't have timed a better entrance. Gerry John and Seamus had just risen from their stools, when the padded-leather double doors came swinging wide open. A horde of lesbian couples came marching into the bar; there were those that had taken on a more masculine specific gender role; along with women that could've escaped off the covers of ladies' fashion magazines; one or two were dressed in tailed tuxedos, like penguins; another in an outfit consisting of purple leotard, fiber-optic-lit tutu, a set of iridescent wings like a dragonfly, or a fairy, strapped upon her back...

III

Gerry John, along with Seamus, pushed their way past the eclectic crowd. The odd duo went through the large double doors, music once again pumping, then soon becoming muffled as the doors swung back closed. Seamus followed Gerry John down into the art gallery. It seemed quitter than it should have. Darker, too. The creepy, over-powering sculptures were blazing electric-purple, now. Except for the eye-sockets; 3 witch-green lights floating in tar-pits—

"Ah, pretty strange stuff, don't'cha think?" Gerry John asked Seamus, while giving the sculptures a sideways glance. "Me, I like strange stuff, personally, it reminds me of home."

Seamus said, "Ireland? These things remind you of Ireland?"

"No, not Ireland... Home, laddie."

"But, I thought you were Irish?"

"Oh, I spent a long, long, time in Ireland, but I'm not from there..."

"Where are you from?"

"Someplace ye've probably never heard of."

Gerry John turned on a heel, walking down the stairs, stairs that remained as quiet as could be. Then

Seamus began down the stairwell, the first tread squealing under the pressure of his foot...

Seamus was grateful for the clean, cool evening air, when he finally made his exit from 'Koda.

Bright white twinkle-lights had just started flickering on, in the trees overhead, all along Oceana Avenue. The electric street lights, fashioned to look like old Victorian gas lamps, had yet to light. Gerry John took in a huge lung-full of the night air, seeming to expand in size. Now that he was standing next to him, Seamus was shocked at what a large man Gerry John actually was. He seemed jovial enough, though, so Seamus followed him as he walked down Oceana Avenue. He didn't remember Gerry John having a walking stick, but he had one now; a gnarled branch with its knobby end carved like a forked-tongue skull. The odd couple continued on for the entire length of the open air mall, striding away from the ocean, eventually coming to the tower-like structure of the town clock. In a park, across the street from the clock, there was a fountain; the fountain had a tall obelisk in the center, with an apparatus spraying water in a fine fan of mist. Gerry John physically stopped Seamus with his arm, pointing out the fountain.

"Do ye see the rainbow, Seamus?" Gerry John asked him, his too-long finger still pointing towards the fountain. There, in the mist, was a prism of colors.

"I do." Seamus replied, wondering if he'd mentioned his strange obsession with rainbows over the last few days to Gerry John, during their conversation at the bar. He was sure he had not.

"Now, look over to yer right, just where the rainbow ends," Gerry John told Seamus. A low bluff, maybe a 20-foot elevation, rose up from Oceana Avenue. Perched on that bluff, a large plot of land; sitting on that, a single house. Being just passed dusk, and facing away from the ocean, the bluff *and* house, were little more than a single silhouette; The house only distinguishable from the hill, by the cheery yellow light coming from the lit windows. From where they stood, the house appeared to sit at the end of the rainbow, "That's my house. Me and the Mrs., we run a little bed and breakfast. Rainbow's End, we call it. We don't get all that much business, but then again, we don't exactly need it, so I guess we get what we get and I should be happy about that. At least that's what the Mrs. tells me. Come on, let's go get yer coins!"

As they began walking towards the bluff, they passed the fountain. In what *had* to be an optical illusion of some sort, Seamus told himself it seemed as though the rainbow prism had switched, so that the house was still somehow sitting at the far end of the rainbow's spectrum; deep purple.

After another few minutes walking, the faux-gas lights began flickering to life, one by one. Seamus could see his shadow, wavering out in front of him as he walked; but of Gerry John's shadow, he could see none. Seamus' neck hairs stood up on end. But the lure of gold was even stronger than his voice of reason.

"Where are you *from* Gerry John?" Seamus suddenly brought the subject up again. "You said I've probably never heard of it, but then again maybe I have. Try me?"

"All right then, laddie, seeing as how we're becoming such fast friends, and all," Gerry John began, "I know everyone assumes, because of the accent, that I'm Irish, from Ireland. I understand, I'd probably make the same mistake if I were in yer shoes," Gerry John continued, "but, the place I'm from, is much older than Ireland. So much older. It's much older than humanity, in fact. Home is a land called Fey. A place called Unseelie, to be precise."

Gerry John was right; Seamus had never heard of it. It sounded French. Maybe it was near Rene-la-Château. Maybe this guy's family had found the Templar treasure, rumored to have been buried there... Seamus had read all kinds of books on the Templars that he'd checked out from Pelican Bay's Library. He was a bit of a buff on the subject...

They came to a set of switchback stairs, carved out of the limestone hillside. Seamus followed Gerry John up. At the top, they came out of a dense cluster of trees, revealing a gravel path that lead to the house. To say the setting seemed like something out of a fairy tale, would not be amiss.

The gravel path was well groomed; lined with giant, bright green, wide-reaching ferns. The plant beds were filled with Clover. Amongst the Clover, planted in orderly clusters, were various types of Iris, colorful and jewel like. Behind the ferns, wide strips of lawn, fiery-leaved Maple trees planted perhaps every 30 feet. There was a dozen on each side, lining the path.

As the path crunched to an end beneath their footfalls, Gerry John led Seamus to a neat little iron fence; maybe 3 feet high, covered in whimsical and fantastic designs, surrounding the perimeter of the entire house. Off to left-hand side, was a large wooden sign hanging from an iron bracket. The rings, holding the sign to the bracket, were creaking in the breeze. The sign, read: Rainbows End. Plain and simple. The sign seemed rustic, and very old, of the variety Seamus imagined hanging outside medieval taverns, or Irish Pubs. A smaller sign hung on a smaller set of rings, attached to the bottom, that read: Vacancy.

The house itself was odd. There was no single architectural style that defined it. Instead, it appeared to be a hodgepodge of so many different eras, lending it a funky charm all its own. Seamus thought to himself how he'd just hit a gold-mine, literally; And, for his third wish? He was going to wish for a place to flop for the night.

"Whad'd'ya'say we get right down to diggin', Seamus?" Gerry John stopped short of opening the gate, "I'll show ye the back half o' the property, I've got a place down there, with a hundred coins in a Mason's jar, buried under a willow tree. I've got 'em buried all over this backyard," Gerry John said with insane glee, rubbing his too-long hands together, in a miserly fashion, "Let's go, I've got a shovel back there, by the pool."

Gerry John and Seamus walked along the iron fence, then turned down a side path that led through a tunnel of foliage. Just as Seamus was wondering if the path was ever going to end, they came out into a giant clearing. Gerry John's property must've taken up almost the entire bluff. The whole clearing seemed like a struggle between neat, orderly gardening, and wild botanical insanity. The sheer madness of the place was breathtaking. It was absolutely beautiful. Gerry John went sprinting off over a large patch of manicured lawn, in the direction of what Seamus would've called a large natural pond, not a pool. Seamus started off after Gerry John. Gerry John called back over his shoulder at Seamus, "Be careful not to step on the rings of toadstools. They're fairies' ring's, ye know?" For a man that had claimed to be no spring chicken, he sure seemed spry enough to Seamus. Seamus caught up to Gerry John at the edge of the pool, near a large cluster of boulders. The pool, as Gerry John had called it, was covered in a thick layer of pond scum. Water lilies sat nestled in the thick green algae. Here and there, a large boulder broke the water's surface. Off to the side was a shovel, planted straight in the ground. Gerry John pulled the shovel, buried as deep as it could possibly go, straight up and out of the earth with one hand. He handed the shovel to Seamus and told him, "Follow me."

They walked towards a small shed, around the corner passing it, then continuing along for a few more yards. Gerry John and Seamus stood near the back fence of the property. In the center of the properties fence line, the most gnarled weeping willow Seamus had ever seen. It appeared to have a sleeping, malevolent face. Gerry John walked up to the tree, stopping at arm's length, then reached out to touch the tree with his fingertips. He turned in 180° circle, and paced out 7 steps; toe to heal, toe to heel, toe to heal, toe. Using his foot, at the tip of his toe, Gerry John made an X in the lawn.

"It's right there, Seamus, but it's down in there deep in Mother Earth's belly," Gerry John said, "so no robbers could get to it." He gave Seamus a wink, his malamute eyes seeming to glow in the night, that feral animal-like smile, back on his face. "So why don't ye get to diggin? The sooner done, the sooner I can have a Guinness."

Seamus would have to work one of *those* into part of his third wish, too. Still not sure if this was real; an elaborate prank; or, even worse yet, a dream; For all Seamus knew, he could wake up behind bars; There was only one thing to do. Seamus struck the spade into the rock-hard earth, stomping on it with his right foot, then hopped up on to the rim of the shovel with his left foot. He tilted all his weight back, using the shovels long handle as a fulcrum. He was disappointed at the small clump, mainly grass, that he deposited with disgust onto the ground beside the beginnings of his hole.

Seamus struck the earth again, depositing an equally pathetic amount of grass, and dirt, atop his puny mound. This was repeated over and over, a countless amount of times.

After what felt like an hour of digging, Seamus stood in a hole up to his waist, huffing and puffing. He was sweating balls. Suddenly, off in the distance, he heard a huge splash; Surely something the size of an alligator, Seamus thought, remembering the pool. Gerry John casually swung his glance in that direction.

"Must be the Mrs., going for an evening swim. These October nights can get mighty muggy, here in El Cruz. Jenny just loves swimming in the water." Gerry John mused. Seamus couldn't believe that *anyone* would be willingly to swim in that scum infested pond. Once his breathing had settled down, and the sweat began to turn chill upon his skin, Seamus began digging again; wondering if he would ever strike gold. It was dark now, but his eyes had adjusted to the light; or lack thereof. He'd barely noticed when first 1, then 2, 3 and then 4… Eventually, a dozen bobbing little lights illuminated the scene! Looking up into the branches of the giant weeping willow, Seamus saw what appeared to be giant fireflies dancing there, in the air. Seamus had never seen fireflies before. He continued digging. The fireflies gave off more light and he would have ever thought possible. After digging for what seemed like another hour, at the very least, Seamus heard the sound of breaking glass. Now in up to his shoulders, he brought the shovel up and out of the hole, depositing its contents next to the 4th massive pile of earth he'd created. As he pulled the shovel away, he caught the glimmer of gold from the fireflies' lights dancing above. Off on the lawn, in the direction of what Gerry John had called 'fairies' ring's', Seamus heard the ring of clear bright laughter; like tiny silver bells. Seamus reached out, plucking another $20 Saint-Gaudens gold piece from the dirt. Gerry John, rising up from a nearby boulder, walked casually over to the hole. He dropped to his belly, excavating 6 more coins with his spider-like fingers, then handing them to Seamus.

The coins clinked into Seamus' hand; the 7 coins were *so* much heavier than he thought they'd be, "So, that's seven… thirteen more to go." Seamus shoveled out 3 more scoops of dirt. He began sifting through them, gently, to avoid being cut by the broken glass of the shattered Mason's jar. He quickly removed 7 more coins from the turned earth. That was from the first pile alone. He moved to the second, instantly pulling another 3 from that pile. 'Three left,' Seamus thought to himself. Suddenly he was tired. Really, really, tired, "Hey, Gerry John, can I hand you this shovel?"

Seamus told himself, 'You're almost done.'

"No problem, laddie, go on and give that shovel to me." Gerry John said, nodding; his hand, with those too-long fingers, reaching out for the shovel, then swiftly grabbing it away from Seamus. Gerry John asked, "How are ye doing down there, laddie? Ye look so tired, it looks like ye could sleep like the dead, it does?"

Without really thinking much about it, Seamus said, while stuffing the gold coins in his pocket—he'd bent back down into the hole, to fish out his last 3 coins—

"I'm so tired, I wish I could Gerry John. I really wish I could."

"Yet again! Another wish that's not so hard for old Gerry John to fulfill!" Gerry John announced, as Seamus found yet another coin. Gerry John continued, "It's been a real pleasure, playing these games with ye Seamus, and I do mean that," Seamus pulled coin number 19 from the ground, putting it in his pocket. Seamus thrust his hand back into the earth, scrambling about to and fro. He didn't care about the glass. It was like an internal alarm going off in his brain; He came across something that felt like a tree branch. Seamus pulled it out, prepared to throw it out of the pit, over his shoulder; then he took a better look at the object before doing so. It looked like an arm bone. Just as Seamus realized what exactly it was that he was holding, Gerry John's voice low and raspy, claimed, "I grant you yer third and final wish, Seamus O'Toole. To sleep like the dead!" a shadow fell over the money pit.

Seamus looked up, Gerry John's voice rising on the word "dead". Gerry John was poised at the edge of the hole, now nearly as deep as a grave; his body was all twisted and contorted, the shovel raised like a baseball bat. In the next instant, Gerry John the giant leprechaun, creature of Fey, swung that shovel like Barry Bonds. Hey, batter, batter, batter...Suh—wing! In one clean slice, Seamus' head separated from his body, tumbling once, twice, and then a third time, before bouncing a few more times; Then, coming to a rest some several feet away. Like victims of the guillotine, it took Seamus a few minutes for his brain to realize it was separated from his body. All in all, a pretty fucked process! In the first few seconds, after watching his body slump into the hole, now his grave, that he'd dug, Seamus cried out:

"What the hell Gerry John! Why'd you go and do that. I want a do-over, man! I wish my head was still attached to my body…"

"It doesn't work like that, laddie. This is Rainbow's End. This is where purple fades into black. Luckily, were still in the darkest spectrum o' purple here, and not in the True Black. But Rainbow's End *is* a portal, a place where the things that live in the True Black…can break through the barriers o' this dimension if, and when, properly called. And as far as doing this to ye? I didn't do this to ye. This was decreed by the Fates! Those Weird sisters are also denizens of Fey, ye know? Remember yer life's original mantra, Seamus, and this will all be a little bit easier for ye, 'If it weren't for bad luck I'd have no luck at all,' So go on, laddie, and repeat after me…"

***

That Saturday evening, grad student Amanda Marsh, who was working towards becoming a social worker, packed the last of her things in her backpack. She found the With Open Arms house to be super depressing, but it would definitely look good on her resume later. She looked at the clock; it was 10 minutes 'til 7. Amanda grabbed her clipboard, and walked up to her supervisor, Suzanne's, office. Suzanne had been pretty cool to Amanda, and it seemed like she'd really been impressed when Amanda had told her that Ebenezer Marsh, Marshville's original founder, had been her great, great, great-grandfather. Suzanne would probably let Amanda go early, seeing as how it was a Saturday evening, and all. As Amanda made her final approach to Suzanne's office, she could hear that the television was on. Amanda had been here just long enough to know that Suzanne always watched the super lotto pick. She gently rapped on Suzanne's door.

"Come on in."

Amanda walked into the small, tidy space. She held the clipboard out towards Suzanne, "Hey, Suzanne. We were supposed to have 3 new admissions today, but only 2 of them actually showed. The guy that didn't show was O'Toole. Seamus O'Toole. So, we give him another 48 hours to show, and then we just take him off the list and move on to the next?"

"Yeah Mandy," Suzanne had taken to calling Amanda, Mandy, "that's pretty much the way it works.

You can call ma Suze, you know. And don't go worrying about reporting him to the parole office, that's not our job. That's their problem. With Open Arms just gives them a place to live. You know how bureaucracies work now, don't you, Mandy? Well, *everything* is very, *very*, compartmentalized. You're doing a good job, around here. I mean it. If you want take off for the night, go right ahead. A girl should have a good time on a Saturday night. Say, have you ever gone dancing at 'Koda, up in El Cruz? Ladies' nights are a blast!"

Amanda said no. She was pretty sure Suzanne was hitting on her. She'd never heard of 'Koda. Amanda was a bit bookish, and didn't get out all that much. As Amanda was leaving Suzanne's office, she heard a voice on the TV, announce, "and tonight's winning lottery numbers are... 33... 7... 13... 77... And finally... Number 21!"

***

All over the news the next day, in newspapers up and down California, those numbers would be listed as: 7, 13, 21, 33 and 77. The numbers of a huge lottery, $26 million, that would go unclaimed. Numbers that could be found on the decomposing ticker-tape of a fortune cookie, stuffed in the coin pocket of Seamus O'Toole's pants, along with over $20 thousand worth of gold coins in his other pockets... Oh, poor Seamus O'Toole; who never had any luck but bad luck; who was buried in one of the many, many, *many*, graves... in that backyard, at Rainbow's End.

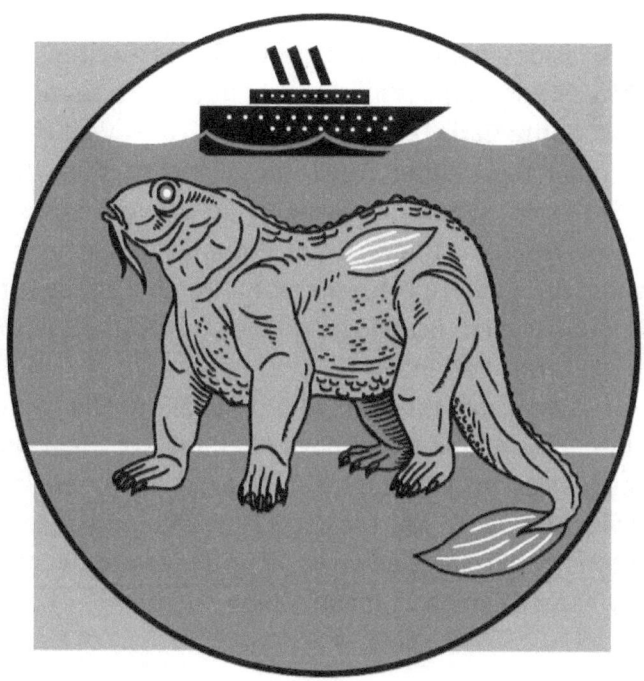

Besides being an illustrator & hack-writer, Mat Fitzsimmons is a fairly odd dude who resides in Santa Carla, er, ah, I mean El Cru—, wait that's not quite right either...Well, uh, all righty, then. Mat Fitzsimmons, when not living in an interdimensional bubble, resides in the very real, though at times surreal, Santa Cruz, California. He shares his humble abode with his kick-ass wife, Brandi, who holds a black-belt in the art of Eternal Patience.

Like most people who dabble in the weird fiction, Mat & Brandi (she does not dabble in the weird, except vicariously through him. She did like the *Hellboy* movies, though!), are the proud parents of a gigantic (at time of bio, she's down to 19 pounds from twenty!) kitty named Cthloe... I mean, Chloe.

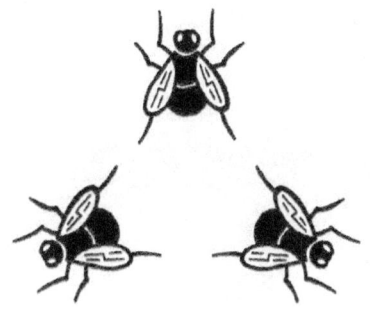

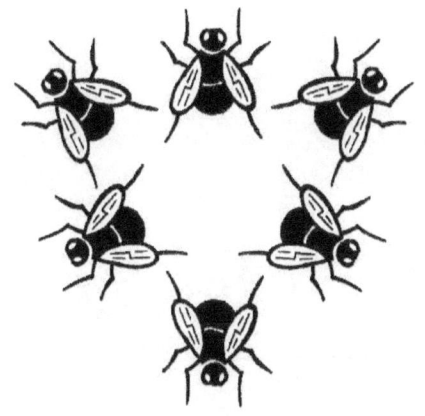

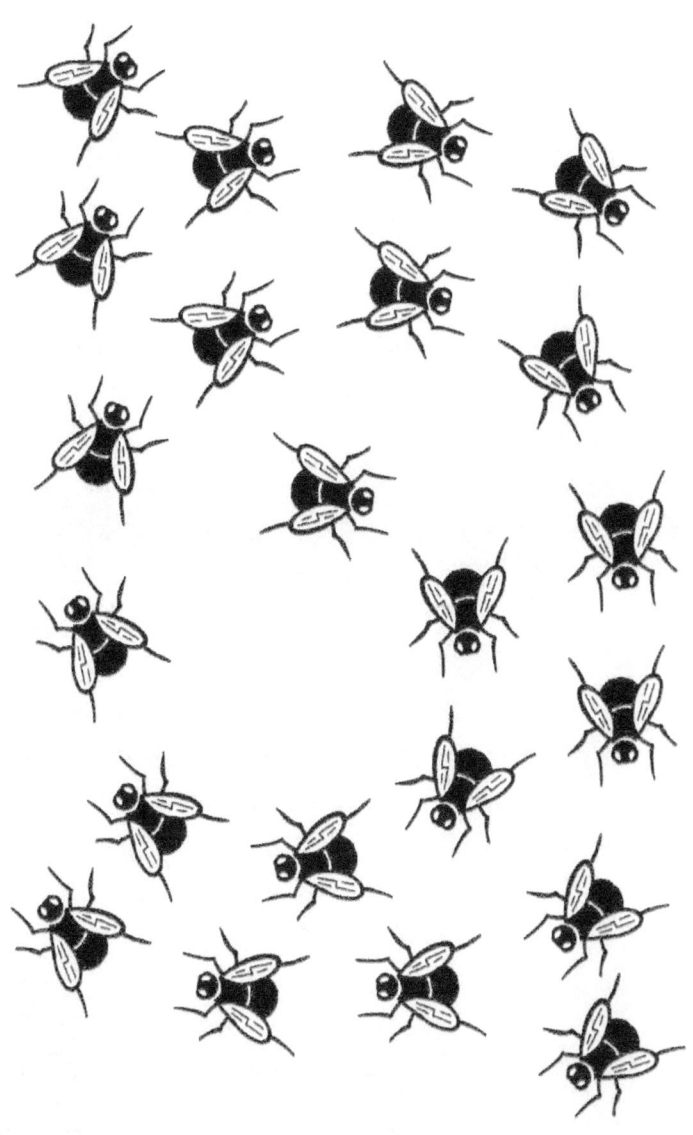

B y Decree of our Highest Office, We, The Esoteric Order of Xushathula, Oh Mightiest of the 7 Queens, The Queens of the Rim of Fire, bestow thanks upon you, dear visitor; Thanks, for helping us bring into existence those Things That Should Never Be Called, for it is in the traveler's imagination, their dreams, that these Terrible, Great Old Ones may still manifest; may still call from unknown chasms; may still hold dominion & sway over the minds of humanity...

We hope you enjoyed your stay in beautiful seaside El Cruz, California. We strive to "Keep El Cruz Weird", as I'm sure you've noticed our proud locals claiming with their bumper-stickers. There are always exciting things going on (even in the offseason!), 'Praise Xushathula!', here in our quaint coastal resort town. We, at The El Cruz Board of Tourism, hope that you tell your family and friends about our charming little seaside resort town; and We, the board, hope to see you all again, sometime real soon...

Our Best Regards,
The El Cruz Board of Tourism

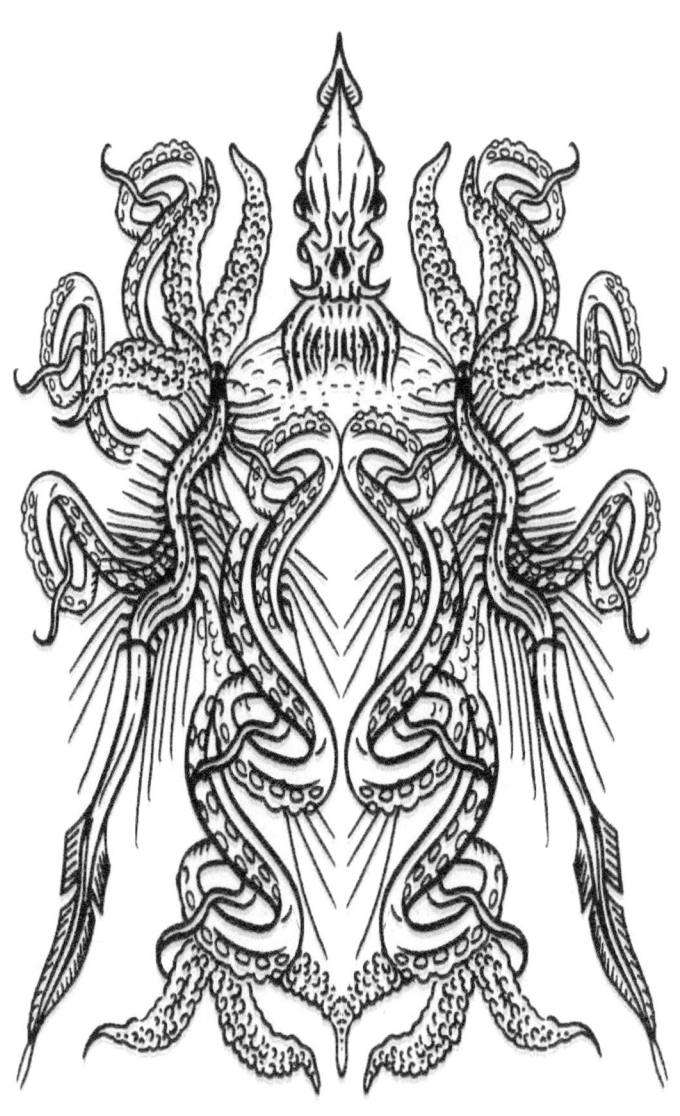